I0716105

THE STILL BEATING HEART OF A DEAD GOD

Sam Richard

For my dad, George Richard (Sept. 14th, 1953 - October 26th, 2024)
Thank you for everything.

For Jes.
The inspiration behind so much of this book.

For Mo.
Missing you always.

CONTENTS

Introduction	ix
The Spiraling Cadaver	1
The Nest Within	11
Body Alone	21
Flesh Crucifix	33
Jizz Christ	43
Portrait of a Red Tower	57
All Alone on the Stage Tonight	71
Meslithe	81
From the Past Comes the Storm	97
The Antecedent	113
The Still Beating Heart of a Dead God	125
Acknowledgments	129
Previous Appearances	131
About the Author	133
Also from Weirdpunk Books	135

INTRODUCTION

A few weeks before this book was slated for initial release my dad died. We knew it was coming eventually, but of course you always think you have more time.

My dad, George as he was known to most, was (among many, many other things) one of my biggest supporters as a writer. Apparently he told a ton of folks about my work. It was always apparent how proud he was of me.

I wanted to repay that, in some small way. This book was to be (and still is) dedicated to him. I was holding onto the hope that it would come out while he was still with us and he would get to see that; to truly know how much his support and impact means to me.

But that didn't get to happen, and while part of my brain wants to run through all the what-ifs about how I could have made this happen before he died, I also know well enough that there is nothing in those thoughts but more pain. Pain without end.

If he's not here to know that this book is dedicated to him and why, then at the very least I can let everyone else know.

I wouldn't be a writer if it weren't for my dad. He was the person who got me into film and comics and reading and thinking about storytelling. From an early age, he had us kids building our own characters for ttrpg campaigns (lots of

D&D, but Chill is the one that I always think back on) and painting their corresponding miniatures. He introduced me to horror, first through a red-shelled VHS copy of the Universal Dracula and later through Evil Dead. I was probably 7. He rented me Conan the Barbarian and Deathstalker around the same time. One of my favorite recurring memories throughout my childhood is simply all the times we went to the movies together.

He bought me occasional birthday subscriptions to The Amazing Spider-Man and X-men comics and got me Alan Moore's Killing Joke for Christmas one year.

He facilitated a love of reading from an early age that I can't even pinpoint where it began. I do know books like Ender's Game and Gary Gygax's Greyhawk series were involved, eventually.

As a pre-teen, we stole his copy of the Simon Necronomicon and tried to summon a great old one in the park down the street from his house. I told him that story a few years ago, explaining that it's why I have a tattoo of the Necrinomicon Gate on my knee, and he just laughed.

I bought my first Lovecraft paperbacks from a thrift store in early high school because I had seen those books on his shelves. About a year later, he bought me my first Harlan Ellison book.

Throughout my life, he would ask what I was reading and tell me what he was currently working through. We often talked books, even the last few times I saw him.

I wouldn't be a writer if it wasn't for my dad. I wouldn't be publishing, I wouldn't be involved in the community, I simply wouldn't be here.

Dad, I'm so sorry that you aren't here to see it, but this one's for you. And really, they all were, even if it took me a while to realize that.

\- Sam Richard

11/13/2024

THE SPIRALING CADAVER

He didn't get to talk with her before she died because he missed her call. He doesn't remember her final message because he was drunk when he listened to–and then deleted–it. Like her final communication with him never happened.

Like she was never here.

And he wonders if maybe that's partially true. That maybe his memory isn't real, or at the very least isn't accurate. That the woman who he would give anything to see one more time had perhaps been more an amalgamation of several people experienced through the haze of alcohol and prescription pills.

Like he was never here.

But neither was the world. Or at least not really. That day the two of them watched another plane drop another bomb and another group of civilians seeking refuge were wiped clean off the map. No. Not clean. Horrifically so, covered in dust and blood and cinder and ash. Found holding each other, trying to huddle in some kind of futile collective notion of safety. Bodies mangled.

Their bones shattered, protruding from their gray flesh. No longer able to experience joy or love or hope or pain or sadness or self-righteousness or anger or greed or lust or friendship. People reduced to the things we were forged from. Clay and dirt and oil. Carbon.

The human stain.

But the day the two of them watched another plane drop another bomb in another country, as they had year after year after year. As they all had. As we all have. Waiting for the planes and the bombs and the sorrow and the fear to finally come to them. To finally come on them.

They sat together, drinking a bottle of cheap corn whiskey she'd picked up on her way home. The delight in her eyes; the delight always in her eyes. But instead they sat in silence once the bombs fell. Seemed like another day of horror, in that way that you might get used to over time.

Exposure therapy, but the dark inverse of that idea.

Numbness.

Inhumanity.

Shock.

Humanity.

Isolation.

Embrace.

They sat on their rickety, itchy couch exhausted from the day, from the week, from the month, and watched those fucking bombs fall. Eternal shall they reign.

They sat in silence. In pained awe. Not the awe of love and acceptance and abstract holy divinity, but awe of a truly biblical kind. Terrible and unknowable. The thing that melts your ability to think for hours or days or weeks or years or decades. Lifetimes. Generations. Centuries.

Just another day.

Always another fucking day. Another fucking bomb.

They watched it hit over and over from different angles like it's high quality porn. The money shot repeated in slow motion on television and on the internet for all the world to see. Look at how well we do this. *Look at how good we are. Look at how we fucking got them, enemies huddling together in their underground bunkers.*

It was too much; it was always too much, and she

slammed another massive glug of the brown liquor and went to bed. Her head was pounding, tears threatening to break the surface tension of her eyelids. The images wouldn't go away. They're always there. If not that night, then the next night. And if not these people, then someone else. Someone who isn't them, but that doesn't make it feel ok. It just makes it empty and horrible and like the whole fucking world needs to stop and spin in reverse just to feel the mammoth weight of everyfuckingthing that it lets happen. That makes it happen. And we don't even pause; we don't hesitate.

The bed was soft and warm but hollow. All creature comforts rotting from the inside while the world remains—insists on being—this way. She cried herself to sleep, hoping for the numbness of exhaustion or booze or grief to take it away, to give her just a goddamn second to breathe without every gasping breath being full of abrasive, carcinogenic dust and irradiated powdered blood.

She could see the gray of their skin, the unmoving muscles underneath and nothing made sense. She fitfully slept with the images of the dead hovering over her, not as ghosts or apparitions, but as fully formed flesh and blood people who once lived and struggled and breathed the same rancid air as her; who once held the door open for a stranger and helped a child who'd tripped on a rock.

They sat with her as she slept.

But he watched the bombs fall. He couldn't rip himself away. Not for her, not for anything. The way that feeling worms its way into your stomach and sends cold blood up to your heart. The way it hurts so fucking much but there's nothing else to do and every single channel and stream and article and video shows the same thing, but it grows increasingly clean and victimless. Our perfect, precise A.I. directed bombs only ever hit their intended targets who are always evil and against us and our allies and what we all stand for. And when they die, they are wiped from the earth like bleach and bacteria, not in a shower of rubble and shrapnel and rockets that shoot out literal knives that sever children's spines at weddings, but in a perfectly ordered way that leaves no trace left behind because there's a movie you should see and a new laptop that you need and are your erections hard enough and how's your testosterone level and didn't this celebrity do something so crazy recently?

That night, he let it shudder through him, moving through his muscles like an orgasm. It hollowed him out, at least what was left to hollow out. Like the entire media-consumer interface was mainlined into him. Freebasing misery and consumer goods and pre-packaged opinions.

He popped another pill and downed it with a quarter of the bottle of whiskey.

The television his lullaby, his comfort, his everything.

The next morning she was gone. Nothing scary, just off to work. He could sense her warm lips on his cheek as he was waking up, as though she had just kissed him and was merely on the other side of the front door. Like she wasn't really gone, would never be gone but for a fleeting moment before they could be together again.

The television was still blaring. New images, new planes, new bombs, new victims. Not sure where. Same battle? Same country? Same American-made weapons - the only thing that leaves no doubts.

He went to the park to walk off some of the hangover, though a fifth of something in his pocket also helped. The cool air burned his lungs. He remembers that still. The way it stung. The way it constricted the tissue, making it harder to breathe like so much coal and burning rubber and melting plastic and toxic fumes.

A couple and their child walked by him, glaring at the bottle in his hand, but he was just glad to see other people around.

Isolation.

Fear.

Xenophobia.

Hate.

Suspicion.

All things perfected in the USA.

The park led to the bookstore and then to a restaurant and then to a bar and another and another and another. Drunk and alone, surrounded by strangers also wanting to connect but no longer knowing how, like the gears of socialization had been plenty lubed by the booze, but were too rusted in place for it to matter.

At least that's how it felt for him.

Another handful of cheap beers and a few more pills, just to take the edge off, and the night went blank.

And then her calls, which he only knows from looking at his phone later. And then her message, which he only knows from looking at his phone later. And some ghost of her voice, but no clue what the words are or if they were even from that night. What if he's mixing together the cadence and rhythm of her voice from so many other conversations? An approximation of her essence.

What if it isn't what her voice sounded like at all. Now misshapen by time and grief and trauma and longing.

He only knows that the next day someone found her body in the woods. Her favorite woods. The deepest part of her favorite park on the far end of town. Dangling from a massive tree. Suicide. Her boots were off, on the ground beneath her feet.

She always loved to be barefoot.

No note.

Just the voicemail.

He panics when he thinks about it too much. When he imagines her alone in those woods, trying to decide if the world was too far gone and had given her nothing but pain and sorrow and misery despite what good there was. The thought of her calling and him not answering. Of that being the deciding factor. The terror rises in his chest and he might pass out or puke or just start running and never stop. Which is what he did.

Only he did stop, at some point.

He popped more pills and downed them with the last of

the liquor and ran until the hysteria in his heart was overrun by the pain pulsing through his body. Too much, too far, for too long, too hard, too painful, too exhausted.

He collapsed.

Woke up some time later. Dead phone. Unsure of where he was, how he got there.

Surrounded by echoing emptiness. And dirty, but still still shimmering tile.

Frozen escalators. Unmoving figures staring at him from behind grimy glass windows. He wanders the corridors, trying to figure out how he's gotten in. The memories so hazy and awful. Her bastard voice over and over in his ears speaking in the indecipherable tongues of a pentecostal preacher.

The way her skin was so gray, just like the planes and the bombs and the buildings and the people crushed beneath them all. The weight of her hand in his, unmoving and unalive and unconvincing in the hope that she would just squeeze back and everything would be ok again.

The mall stretches out in front of him eternally; storefront after storefront, to the point where they all bleed into one another. He tries to recall if he had seen that same sporting goods store ten minutes ago, or if it was a different one, maybe by a different name. Different places, same font.

He tries to memorize each store he passes, taking special effort to say their names out loud to himself and the echo. *Hat Factory, Toys'A'Billion, Rejora, Antiqu, Freedom Clothing, Fjorsons.* Each store different, but he always forgets in about twelve entries what the others had been.

Endless shopping experiences. All gated off and dark inside. All covered in dust and grime. Ash and cinder.

Maybe blood, too.

An abandoned cathedral to our highest religion. He passes an electronics store with one lone high-def flat-screen tv on. More planes, more bombs, more fanfare and reverie. More technology that he holds dead in his pocket helping lead the way. More gray and broken, nameless, faceless bodies. We rarely see the reality of their grief, much less in their joy, their celebrations, in their daily lives. *We got'em!* on the screen. More shit and misery and death and pain and emptiness. More human inhumanity evolving into inhuman inhumanity by way of drones and artificial intelligence. Same blindness, but now with shiny new toys.

The television manufactured by the same company that made the bombs and the planes and the cameras recording it. The same company that owns the store in the mall and the real estate investment firm that owns the mall and has controlling shares in the film studios who are advertising their films on the same televisions network showing the bombs who also own the delicious and refreshing soda advertised after the movie trailer. The film was produced in conjunction with the Pentagon who have final cut rights of the film just so there's nothing subversive in there, but it's worth it because the film company got to use their planes and tanks and aircraft carriers. The same planes that are dropping the bombs. And the heroes smile with perfectly white teeth and nary a spot of blood for the victorious and brave efforts fighting more bad guys halfway across the world.

Her voice distorts more in his ears. Her laugh is gone from his memory.

He keeps going. More filthy glass. More tangles of escalators. So thirsty, he lets the final drop of metallic whiskey tingle his tongue.

Down a few more corridors, to nowhere in particular. To nothing in particular, just hoping for fresh air and the sky overhead. Hitting a center, of sorts, in the mall sits a fountain. The water is thick and congealed with time. Filling up his bottle, he takes a swig. Warm and unappealing, but salty in a refreshing way that makes no sense in his mouth and down his throat.

He pops another few pills and treks forward, into the unknown of the mall. More storefronts bleeding together into others. *Have I been this way before?* His phone vibrates in his pocket. His dead phone.

A voice message. He hits play.

It's her voice again, ringing in his ears. Not a known language. Tongues, gibberish. It's coming from the phone, but filling the empty, endless halls. Her voice meets the echo and they dance across the marble floors, glass, and tile walls. They shimmer in the majesty of acoustics, bounding and bouncing from one corridor to the next.

Like a knife to the soul.

He tries to turn it off, but his phone stares blankly at him. Breathing, speaking, dead. It pulses in his hand like something's crawling through it.

Her echo walks with him. He drinks more of the thick salty water and gags down a couple more pills until the bottle is empty. He tosses it with a skid that joins in the chorus around him.

He walks and walks and walks. *Forest-Mart*, *Pretzel Man*, *Cliniq*, *Vertigo*, *Roberth's Shoes*. A neverending array of options that don't repeat, of this he's sure.

Shifting waves of gray sand blow in across the marble, the wind sharing in the glee of the echo and her voice and the skittering. His movements grow slow and tedious in the heavy grit. Great heat rises from nothing and nowhere. Loud popping in the distance. The shop windows are scuffed and scratched by the abrasive dust, which slowly climbs up the side of the glass, getting higher and higher until it's up to his thighs.

His mind occupied with the everything and the nothing of it all, so much so that he almost misses the open door to one of the shops. *Red Owl*. Mannequins in hiking gear stare out at him from the doorway and through the glass. Entering, he closes the door behind him, trying to stop the slow pour of sand from gaining any more ground in the relatively unscathed outdoors store.

The echo isn't as loud in there, but her voice still drones, reduced back to what it was before the mall. The incessant cry to be heard, the mystery within his own fragile mind. The specter that will never leave.

The droning of a television from the other side of the

room. Slowly, he follows, trying to keep his focus on signs of life for the first time since he arrived.

How long has it been? Could they be opening soon? Maybe a chance to find someone who knows where an exit is. But are they open at all? Is there a 'they' who are coming?

But then fear, coiling up underneath the questions, pushing down his throat like so many filthy, jagged fingers.

More planes and more bombs and more buildings and more people turned to nice, clean dust before a snapshot of how this soda will save the world if someone were to only listen and that massive gasoline companies are doing their best to keep the environment safe and clean and how exciting it is that your favorite corporate banking institutions now has queer friendly commercials and don't you love it and maybe you should join the Marines, you are a real man after all, aren't you?

Something moves behind the tv. Frozen, unsure what to do, he wants to call out, but he can't hear himself over her voice and the incessant bombs and gray-skinned children being carried by their broken wailing mothers and this delicious new taco is available up until 3:00 AM at the drive-through and why didn't he just answer the fucking phone and why didn't he just answer the fucking phone and why didn't he just answer the fucking phone and up next on the news are your children in danger—here's how—and why doesn't he remember her last message and why can't he understand her words and why the fuck did she die oh god why did she fucking kill herself what the fuck did I do why is this happening and you should invest in gold and I just want her to be here again even if it means we can't be together I just need to know that she can be out existing in the world living her life in hope and dreams and love and pain and hardship and all the things that come with being alive but what the fuck this shouldn't be part of it and can she just come back and I'll take her place I don't even fucking care I just want it all to end.

And maybe it does.

And maybe it doesn't.

Because he'll never know because I'll never know and we keep doing this over and over and nothing fucking changes. More death. More shiny new weapons. More new sneakers to buy. More endless fucking malls invading our waking lives. None of it meaningful. None of it necessary.

Just like her death.

And several figures appear, covered in camping clothing with the tags still on. They don't speak. They just observe. Their attention split between him and the images on the television and their phones. The high-def flat-screen that pulses with comfort and warmth, that invites him in to join them just as they invite him in to join them. Not with words. Unspoken warmth. Unspoken comfort. The videos on their phones flash in unison with each other. With the television. One broken image at a time.

And he's not alone. They bask in the unnatural glow and watch the shiny planes and their funny bombs and the cartoon villains who get hurt but come back week after week with more new hijinks and plots. And there is no dust or blood or shattered lives or dead children anymore. There is only warmth and comfort and light.

THE NEST WITHIN

She writhes and contorts slowly, freezing in time on occasion, as if she were glitching out. Maybe the connection is bad, a narrow buffer between the live-stream and the action in front of the camera. All that information sent through a signal in the air, then hardwired down into the depths of the earth, all before coming back up, spitting back into the air, and displayed on the screen in crystal clear quality. Or at least that's how it should have gone.

Instead she clips in and out of movement. Sometimes repeating back minute action she'd already taken. Like watching a chameleon walk across a branch. Slow. Reverse imitating the trajectory of their limbs. Alive, but almost unalive. Like a character in a dying arcade game.

She's alive. Not unalive at all. Shimmering sweaty skin on the other side of the world, or just the other side of the block. No way of knowing. Her moans real; or real enough to get the job done. Human at the very least.

Her self-exposure, somehow more intimate than seems normal. Not just seeing her body, not just seeing those parts generally kept between lovers, but seeming to bare an essential portion of herself in the act. In this act. Whatever it actually is.

She moves up and down on the toy, vigorously. Animalistically. In that way that makes you breathe heavily even though you want to remain cool, composed. In a way that makes you see stars and heightens the sensation of your heart pounding in your chest.

The blood swells.

It's never like this. Not with the separation of a screen, of the tangled wires below. This is what it's like with someone real. With someone here, in the room. And it almost feels like it. Like she's in here, breathing heavily with you—into you. Her warmth and strength and grace and pure eroticism funneling not just into your eyes, but penetrating your soul.

But she glitches again. She's moving both forward and backward at once, both where her body was and will be all existing at the same time. You don't want to miss anything. You don't want to rob yourself of whatever this is, but every single time you get close, every single time you can hear her moans vibrate through your skin, the glitching gets worse.

And worse.

And worse again. Compounded and fractured.

So you reset the wi-fi, hoping it won't take all of 5 minutes to get back to normal. Praying that it's just an issue on your end and not an issue on hers. Or the server. Or the hosting company. Or your provider. Or somewhere, deep in the wires. The blood dissipates while you wait, now less aroused and more anticipatory. More curious.

But could she be on this block? In this city? The state? The country? Would it matter if she lived next door.

But it feels like she knows you, like she's peered deeply into all your fears. Strangely. You know you've only lurked, never typed a word, but when she stares into that camera it's like she's speaking to you. To every part of you. Microcosmically.

Wi-fi is still resetting and you feel like a fool. Like a child. Like the kind of person who expects everything be given to them. The entitlement of another's love. But you swear this is different. This isn't some incel shit. *Right?* It's a connection. A new thing, not weird ass behavior from a nutjob online. Inside, she's calling to you.

The icon flashes a few times and she's back on the screen. Upon refresh nothing has changed, aside from her position, now on her back, long legs in the air, arm at her side, reaching around her hip to push the toy in and out and in and out. The refreshed urgency of arousal runs down your spine. But she's still doing it; moving unnaturally. Like a spider gently plucking at strings on a web to make sure they're taut and pulling back to pluck again. She's shifting. Phasing almost, but still here.

Still crawling into you. Into those secret places you have buried deep inside that you never show anyone. That you've never allowed another into. All parts of her stare at you from the screen. She's rooting around in there, re-wiring and bending the circuits.

Her movements flow arrhythmically; her shadows following closely, but not too closely. A blurred line around her that mirrors and drags. She's cutting through the air. She's penetrating everyone watching. It's perfect. Comfortable. Intimate in a new, unknowable way.

Before she climaxes, before you can climax, the feed cuts to black. Your heart drops in your chest, hitting your stomach and sending cold rushing through your veins. Disappointment yes, but also grief, somehow. *Grief?* Yes, grief. Deep sorrowful mourning. You try to shake it off but it's already sunk in. The cursor hangs over the close button, but you notice that the feed hasn't gone silent. Just dark.

Like someone threw something over the camera or turned off the lights.

The wet sound of penetration still pours from the small laptop speakers, barely edging out your own panicked heartbeat in rattling your ears. The sorrow is gone, but apprehension has taken its place. What previously felt like a free-exchange of sexual activity between consenting adults now seems grimy and wrong. Does she know the feed is still live? Is this a part of the performance?

Sitting at the precipice between elation and trepidation gives you goosebumps and a new, and intense, energy crawls across your genitals. Almost primordial in urgency, you go to work on yourself, setting the cadence of your pleasure to the sounds of hers. It doesn't take long before you're spent.

Delirious.

Exhausted.

Content.

Darkness pulls you deeper into your chair and you pass out to her wet sound still radiating around you. It follows you into your dreams.

Wires pulling at you from below. The corpse of a fox in a darkened alley, decaying fluids running out its mouth, into a sewer grate. A soft hand on your thigh; maybe too close, but also comfortable and reassuring. Veins on concrete, shuddering at your touch. An up-close mouth, slurping raw meat off of bones. Being surrounded by cold flesh. Then, darkness.

The birds are cawing outside the window of your cramped single-room apartment when you come to. It's still a little dark out, but the early morning sun is threatening to crest over the horizon line. You clean yourself up in the bathroom and come back to the laptop, awakening it from its sleep. Crust still in your eyes.

The window is still open to the cam-site, but she's gone. Mild slopping noises fill your ears, but they aren't coming from the speakers. It's hot. So hot you're dizzy. Like being way too high.

A quick search on the history bar of your cam account shows nothing. You haven't watched anything all night. Or the day before. You double check that you aren't logged out, but you are so it should be there. Nothing. No viewing history. Maybe they had a server crash. Browser history is the same. Nothing for the past 2 days. *The fuck.*

What was her handle, *Sleaze-something-13*? Nothing comes up. You try everything you can think to fill the 'something' spot. Nothing works. Empty. *The fuck was the 'something?'*

Search and search and search. Frustration and anger and abject terror.

She was real. It was real. A mantra over and over in your mind.

The blood pools.

A pat pat pat sound and dampness on your sweating neck and shoulder. Blood on your hand. It's coming from your ear. The squishing drone gets louder until something pops. But there's no pain. A pressure release. Still just a trickle of blood. The sound is gone. Still the birds outside, singing to the rising sun.

Still the blood.

You clean yourself up again in your grimy bathroom and throw on a pair of not clean but not too dirty pants and a fresh shirt. The room is off. The floor shifts under you, as if it's breathing. Snake-like veins crawl inside the wood across the floor. One underfoot and you yelp. It reacts to your touch. Like arousal.

The door slams behind you as you run from the house.

Fresh air.

Food.

Reality.

The world is suddenly so bright. Crystalline in intensity. Vibrant and horrible smells fill your nose. It's beautiful and awful and you can't stop shaking. Trembling.

The pat pat pat is happening again. Blood collects, staining your shirt. Squicky sounds fill your ears, but at a low level. Nothing pops. You're still so hot. Sweating through your shirt.

Bitter, old coffee and stale donuts are the order of the day, bought at the gas station around the corner. Cameras are everywhere, watching. Would it feel different if they were just listening? You imagine them covered with a fluid-stained towel. The blood swells.

She dances in your mind, profanely. Beautifully. Your heartbeat increases, walls of your blood vessels hard against the quickly flowing blood. Rigid in all possible ways.

Her sound, no longer in your ears, but off in the distance. The pain of separation, as though you've known anything but in your life. But it isn't just isolation and loneliness, it's a severed response, deep in the lizard brain. Like life was stolen. Love was stolen. Connection and oneness and unification with the fucking universe. Once there and now gone.

In the blink of an eye.

The sound fades. Panic sets in.

Why are they all staring? But the street is mostly empty. Someone drives by and they pay no attention to you. But the cameras see. On every building. Ogling. Peering. Surveilling.

Feels like a bad trip, but you haven't had drugs in years. Outside is fucked, so you go back home. Not satisfied. Not anything but broken.

Back to the computer. Desperate searches on every social media. *She has to have one.* Every search engine. Various configurations of the *something* word with additional search tags. *Model. Sex worker. Cam girl. Alt-model.* Old school message boards you haven't been to since high school that somehow still exist, naming names, sharing and selling images and videos culled from private cam shows and fansites. The bottom end of the trade. Rats and snakes making a buck selling unknowing people's work. Selling unknowing people's bodies and souls to waiting masses of scumbags.

It leaves you hollow.

She's not here. She's not anywhere. A digital ghost. And so she haunts.

The floor trembles beneath. Root-like veins gently spread toward the door. And once out there, they spread down the hall. Then down the steps, out the door to the building. And onto the street, toward the small downtown. Wood and carpet and concrete and blacktop, all shiveringly alive.

The wetness squishes in your ear and you follow the veins. Let 'em watch. Smashed beer bottles, mysterious stains on the cement, and discarded rotting food litter the street. The cacophony of smells and sensations isn't gone, just dimmed by her call.

On an empty street corner a few cops drive by, sirens blaring. Early for an emergency, or maybe late for one. Across the street, a park. Fairly empty, taking up a city block. Scattered park benches and some small grassy hills with a smattering of trees comprise the whole thing.

A couple early morning joggers and a few folks sleeping on the benches are all the life the park holds. But in the small cluster of woods you spot her.

Not scantily dressed, but in smart business wear. The kind that tries to suppress the passion, but can't quite conceal it. Or that's what you tell yourself at least. The blood swells. It now trickles from your ear. Her sound becomes crystal clear.

Heart palpitates like it's flip-flopping. Maybe skips a beat every now and then from pounding too erratically, too powerfully. She doesn't notice you. But you want her to. But maybe you don't. Maybe it's better to know what she's doing. Or who she is. Or how she's even here.

This small city. Damn near the same block. *How*.

She spends a moment in the trees, the subtle glitch tracing after her movements. Mirroring them, but profane and unnatural. It's impossible to tell what she's doing. Suddenly she's off, walking quickly toward the other side of the park, her shadow too close and too far all at once. She's on the next block by the time you reach the edge of the trees. Hurried pace, but needing to keep some distance becomes the struggle.

Buildings grow more derelict as you get closer to the edge of the city. Not much life out here. Beyond is the oil-slick river surrounded by rows of dead and dying trees and piles of littered trash. Abandoned factories and crumbling warehouses. Remnants of a strong working class now diminished to little more than rust flakes and black & white photos that hang in the corner offices of the upper-middle class.

Bombed out, burned up; chewed and spat out. This is America.

Unsure if she's noticed you following or not, she gets lost in the cluster of industrial remnants. You hung back too much, let her get away. The fear sets in. So does the grief. Blood now flows from your ear for a moment before the cement ripples below and leads you closer, into one of the forsaken warehouses.

Dusty piles of rebar-penetrated cinder litter the vast roofless building. She disappears down a set of steps in the middle of the debris. Her shadow follows after, slightly delayed. Her movements strange and unnatural as she descends.

Glitchy and off. Worse and stranger than before.

As quietly as you can, you follow. Through the tattered warehouse and down the filthy steps. Her wetness echos in the darkness below. Moans raise the hairs on your neck.

The blood swells.

The blood also pours from your ear. Slick like oil but quickly growing tacky like drying honey. Shirt soaked in thick red fluid and sweat. Ears full of wetness—both in sound and in blood.

Light on. A single room below the center of the massive building. Her room.

The bed she was on; same comforter, same antique brass frame headboard behind. Laptop sitting open. Hastily placed paintings. Lingerie and sex toys scattered around. A ravenous scent in the air.

Squishing and moaning, but the room is empty. A webcam sits on a desk near the edge of the bed. You go to look at the computer, for lack of knowing what else to do.

But the blood has been draining for so long. Lightheadedness damn near takes you to your knees. Head and eyes full of stars.

Reality rushes back and you're in your own room again. Nighttime. Laptop open and she's vibrating, skipping through space in that irreal way. Glitch but made flesh.

The blood pumps and swells. Ear still bleeding, but it's of no consequence. She's here again. On screen it's a solo chat. No one else. No watchers, no annoying commenters. Just you and her.

Finally. You and her.

Part of you knows it makes no sense, but it also makes all the sense in the world. Everything you've ever wanted—wait, is this it? *Everything?* But the thoughts fade fast. She's on her knees, ass to the camera. Her neck strained so she can stare back at you—into you—at the same time. She's inviting you in. Open. Wet and warm and so comforting.

Yes. Everything you've ever wanted. *Everything.*

You sit down in front of her, blood swelling with a pressure previously unknown to your body. It fights against your veins and runs from your ear. Your face to the screen, up against her skin. But also actually up against her skin. It's bizarrely cold, but so warm and inviting. Watching yourself on the screen put your face in her ass. Also being the one on the screen—the one in the room—putting your face in her ass. The squishing sound permeating your every molecule.

The chill of her touch courses through your flesh and bones and muscle and blood. Sweet, hot blood. And it's swelling. So tight it might pop and leave you deflated on the ground of your filthy one room apartment, but also on the ground of her room. On the floor of the room on the screen.

And the way she moves, back and forth in an unknowable cadence. Mirroring her own movements. It makes no sense on the screen and it makes no sense in front of you in the room. But it worms through you, radiates out of you and you're doing it too. Both in your room and on the screen in front of you, as you watch yourself touch her. Splitting down the middle.

Fractured selves both existing in one feedback loop of boiling hot pleasure, chilling touch, and sensations so deeply embedded that they may never come out. It feels so fucking good. Like you could fuel the world with this energy if only it was catchable. Containable. Sensual and erotic, but beyond all that as well. Magnetic. Complete pole reversal. Negative to negative and positive to positive, but both repelling and attracting all at once. And the movement within that sticking close to you like a shroud.

Her moans move through your, shaking your core. Shattering a foundation deep within. You were right. There was a connection back there, on the screen before; now on the screen and in her room. Unspoken for fear of spoiling it. Unanswered for fear of ruining it.

But it's real. Her cold skin grinding against yours. The way you connect and disconnect and reconnect through so many channels like inputs and outputs. The floor below you ripples with pleasure waves in approximation with hers. You shift and lean into it, pushing further into her. Pressing against all her openness. Begging her to swallow you whole. To consume your very being so you can be united forever.

There is no resistance. She draws you in. Both the you in the flesh, pulled deeper and deeper into the cold crevasses of her body, and also the you in your apartment, pulled deeper into the screen; plastic cracking and adjusting, stretching to make room to fit all of you.

Both halves are pulled further in and down, below the known worlds. Somewhere deep inside. The places that feed us and teach us and give us gifts like fear and passion. Below the confines of knowledge and understanding. One half fleshy and cold. The other half plastic and hot. A tangle of slick wires. A plasma-coated chamber. Both breathe and pulse. Both hum and squish and moan. Both are salvation and comfort.

In both, we are home.

BODY ALONE

The faraway echo of a hollow drum throbbed across the ashen sky as The Man With No Tears walked. No. Not walked: waltzed. He waltzed between acidic pools of oily water and piles of derelict heavy machinery gently humming to himself. Not a melody. Not a tune. But a whirring rhythm of off-kilter ventilation hisses and the impact of pipes clanging together. He did this to the pulse of the distant, cavernous beat.

No sun had been seen in weeks, but that didn't stop the heat of the day from rising through the sodden earth beneath his feet. With every step, he sank just a little further, yet he also floated above the fray. Leather dress shoes both soiled and pristine; wool pant cuffs both soaked and dry. The Man With No Tears' face carried both a smile and a grimace. His humming never broke.

He reached a car on fire, the seats were vacant. There was no driver at the wheel. His body had surely been consumed by the terrible machine. The same terrible machine that would one day come for them all. The Man With No Tears was nearly comforted by the thought. A point of finality, of some kind of cosmic restitution. The inevitability of it all.

Flames gently licked the porous skin of his face. He felt nothing. He was nothing. But then a mild wave of pleasure tickled up his spine. He saw the blaze and the absent driver and the terrible machine awaiting him at the end and his skin grew tight with gooseflesh. He slowly dipped his toe into a shallow puddle, his leather shoe hissing and bubbling for a moment. A gentle moan escaped his lips, but his humming never broke. This was something new.

Sensation.

From a close distance, over the cacophonous drum and his own humming, the screaming of children and a shrill cry pierced through the semi-vacant lot. The hourly ash was starting to rain, burning tiny holes in his peacoat, but he headed toward the shriek to investigate. A gaggle of hyper kids nearly collided with him as he rounded the corner of a dilapidated fence. Most of their hands were smeared black, though one was coated in thick red syrup.

The Man With No Tears smelled it before he saw it. The acrid taste of singed flesh and burnt hair. Just like dinner waiting at home. At his feet, encased in a shell of slowly hardening tar was the body of a cat. A wire was wrapped around it, cutting into the flesh of its neck. The cry shuddered to a stop. The last of its breath hissed out with relief.

If he could feel he would be sad, angry, and broken all at once. If he could cry the tears would be a mix of rage and sorrow. But he could do neither. So there were none.

Gently, he tapped the brick of cat with the same foot he'd dipped into the acid. Warmth radiated off of the poor beast, irritating his already blistered toe. And he understood the pain. The discomfort. Sensations left abandoned for far too long. The ones he thought he no longer had. The kind the world had worked out of him over the years; his nerves dulled to nothing. The grey growing inside and out, consuming everything.

It had always been like this. But it hadn't always reflected so deeply within. At some point, in the far distance of his memories, he could vaguely recall sensations. Ghosts of whispers of dreams told only in negative. Or was this the negative?

Was the gritty black and white that echoed through his life and relationships and home and work and community and city and planet charred by remembrances of something else? An inversion of it all?

Were they all haunted by dreams unimagined?

He stared at the brick cat and wondered.

The drum still throbbed over the day and the cat still hissed its last breath and his humming—his endless fucking humming—never ceased but he could finally remember, or maybe he couldn't, but he could imagine. Imagine this all in beautiful but terrible inverse, or reverse, or transmutation. The ghost memory didn't last long, but it was there. And enough that he couldn't let it go.

In a weak mimicry of misremembered humanity, The Man With No Tears bent down and tried to scoop up the wire-slung, tar brick cat. The wire was stuck to something so he pulled and pulled and pulled to no avail. The hiss didn't alter or pivot in movement, it just kept going. Trying to get some leverage, The Man With No Tears pressed his foot against the fence and gave it a tug. The wire dug further into the cat's neck, but eventually released from the fence with a metallic pop.

Painstakingly, he then carefully unwrapped the wire from the brick cat's neck, careful to not let it dig any further. Once it was clear, the inner most layers of the still cooling tar slowly sealed the crevasse, like the healing of a wound.

Now free of attachment, the creature was still, but its cry continued. He brought the brick cat closer to his face and realized that its whine matched his off-kilter hum; it matched the droning beat of the distant drum.

Unsure of why, he put his chapped and blistered lips to the hardened shell on the cat's head and kissed. Something else shifted inside of him. Not the same as the searing sensual pain of acid or warm pleading burn on his blistered toe, now with its own cooling dollop of tar, but a different kind of sensation. Warmth of a different variety.

It made him uncomfortable. Which was also new.

He inhaled deeply of the commingled city smog and tar stench. It grounded him back to the grit and familiarity of his surroundings. He was struck with a tiredness he had never known so he took his new pet and headed towards home, unsure of why he even went out in the first place. The air around him moved out of his way like curtains as he walked both beneath and atop the sodden soil. He remained both clean and unclean until he reached home.

The Man With No Tears opened the door to his building with a screech and a slam that followed him into his dreams as he and the brick cat fell into his bed. A heavy sleep encased him in a cocoon. Grainy pictures of inverse imagery soothed him as he breathed in the effervescent smog of life. The cat hissed in his arms, its last breath unending. He hummed in his sleep, clanging and whistling in cadence with the distant drums that permeated his drifting mind as a giant clock ticking and ticking and ticking above him. A layer of revulsion dripped on him. It was greasy and cold. The face of the clock kept staring. It kept ticking.

The vibration and noise of trucks regularly heard but never seen shook him awake. Coming to in a panic, he expected to be covered in sweat, but he was drier than coal. As was his cat, still cradled in his arms. His hands were coated in smears of dried tar. *So this is pet ownership?* he thought to himself, blankly.

He put his face to the brick cat and let the hiss of its death-rattle blow across his face. Opening his mouth, he angled it so the hiss moved gently between his teeth, creating a cross-breeze with his incessant hum. There was something unnerving about it, but this new sensation didn't get very deep before he sat up.

Bare brick walls surrounded his rattling bed. Lose bolts shook with every movement of the weathered brass frame and his naked mattress shifted noisily atop the springs below it as he stood. Water ran down the walls perpetually, despite a lack of real rain for what seemed like years. He didn't know if it was broken pipes or an overflowing bathtub in the unit above his. It had been going on for six years, so he had learned to live with it. At the far end of his single-room apartment, the one non-brick wall remained surprisingly dry. Its crumbling plaster was held together by a solitary piece of drooping wallpaper in a fanciful red decorative pattern.

Every time The Man With No Tears stared into it, vague figures inside the markings danced in mocking gestures, so he no longer lent it his gaze despite the pull it had over him. He walked to the far end of the kitchen and looked at his plate, sitting on his makeshift dining table.

Scraps of decaying wool covered both. He brushed them aside, off of the plate. The latter half of a slab of eye-covered potato stared at him. It had been lunch. It had been breakfast. It had been dinner. It had been lunch. It had been breakfast. Going as far back as he could remember. Always under the wool, always covered in the tumorous-looking eyes.

He cut it in half, filling his apartment with the pleasant aroma of singed flesh and burnt hair, and brought the plate to his bed where he set it next to his pet. The brick cat hissed at the food, as it hissed at him, as it continued to hiss with its drying breath. The Man With No Tears pressed a bit of the tuber into the cat's mouth. It hissed through the potato, but some of it appeared to go down. He then ate the other half, a strange sensation of contentment crawling over him for feeding his pet. *This is what you do with a cat*, he thought to himself, confidently.

Perhaps next I should take it for a walk. He was out the door before he had time to wonder if brick cats needed walking, or if they should stay inside.

His door slammed shut, shaking the barren tree at the end of the hallway. It was growing from a mound of sickly-smelling dirt coming up from a tear in the carpet. Leafless, it was almost more an arrangement of sticks than a tree. Every time he walked past it he thought about watering it, but every time he remembered that he didn't have any water. It probably didn't matter anyhow, as the damn thing just kept growing, kept getting bigger.

Once outside, the pair followed some train tracks that went nowhere. He wasn't sure how far to nowhere they went, but he knew it was nowhere eventually.

Nowhere sounded good.

Lost in thought, The Man With No Tears tripped on a crumbling tine and fell to his knees, sending the brick cat clattering across the rocks before it landed in a shallow pool. Astringent gas hit the air with the surface disturbance and the splash glittered silver in the shadows. He crawled to the brick cat, hastily removing it from the puddle.

Gravel and metal shards dug into his knees and palms. He could feel it; truly feel it as it stirred within him.

The tar had drunk in the brackish liquid, deteriorating its surface. Small pills rolled off it as he grasped a hold of the brick cat. His hands were smeared black. They burned with acid, a sensation both debilitating and vaguely erotic. He held that inside, allowing the sensation to bore deep within, feeding the yawning grey and the unending numbness.

But he also feared for his pet. He worked at the brick cat, scraping away the softest layers of tar, hoping at some point he would hit solid again. His hands cried, but he kept working, kept humming. Brick cat kept hissing, not even a minute difference in tone. Eventually he got it to a point that seemed safe enough.

Scraping his hands on the pitted pavement, The Man With No Tears was grateful to have something—someone—to take care of. The tar came off in smears across the ground, gently corroding it. When he was done, he reached down for brick cat, only to find it covered in matte black slugs.

He picked them off one by one, popping them in between his raw fingers. Viscous clear puss oozed out as he squeezed. They smelled metallic. He got almost all of them when one burrowed into the hardened tar. The hole that it left behind slowly closed on its own accord, like a bodily orifice. Unsure what to do, he finished pulling off the rest and threw them into the acidic puddle.

While they hadn't reached any sort of nowhere, he

wondered if it was best to return home, in case brick cat came down with something. He brought it to his face, testing its hiss against his unceasing hum. They sang together like this for a moment and he figured if it wasn't getting quiet or worse, things must be ok.

As The Man With No Tears stood, milky silver blood ran down his shins and palms. It shimmered as it seeped through the porous tar on his hands. Echoes of something moved inside him. Like his burning toe, like his blistered fingers. A sensation fought at the surface of his skin. It drilled deep inside and he shuddered in confusion. Or delight. Or both?

Cradling brick cat, he stood at a vast expanse between his desire to care for the poor creature and a drive to abandon it–and surely himself–to experiencing more profound ways of feeling. This moment was short lived. He had been walking vaguely toward home. But in his state of contemplation he had neglected to stay on the far side of the old tracks leading back from nowhere. They had taken him to the other side of the derelict factories. It may as well have been the other side of the world.

The black planet caught his eye, hovering above. Not exactly out of orbit but also not within. It existed both in the material plane and outside of it. Both possible to see and possible to not see. As he hummed, The Man With No Tears could feel it watching him. Supervising him.

Transgression was fine, but what of feeling?

We're all victims of the oppressive machinery whirring within, whirring below, whirring inside. It takes and takes and takes with its indifference, but it never gives.

The black planet was much harder to see from his neighborhood. It was so clear, so plain, for the first time that he could recall, The Man With No Tears was angry. Not annoyed, not bemused, but sufficiently and horribly angry. A line of fire grew from his throat to his heart. It burned through him like a hot blade. He hummed his rage through squeaking teeth. Static blared in his ears, and for the first time that he could recall, the droning of the drum faded from his mind. His hum briefly wavered, but never stopped.

A harsh new sound echoed from the nearest building. It was quiet at first, slowly building with each repetition. He couldn't place it, couldn't identify it. It was organic. Like there was a softness to it despite its abrasiveness and increasing volume. It was delicately created, but coarse, pulling him closer.

With that his hum shifted. Jagged vibrations worked through him as it synched up with this new sound. It shook him at his core, but he kept walking. Discomfort guided him, gnawing at this freshly unlocked drive. His raw, bleeding hands firmly grasped at brick cat, centering him. *If anything happens to my pet...* he thought to himself, nervously.

The Man With No Tears lifted brick cat to his face, the closest he could approximate to a loving gesture. But for a minute the beast was silent. No more final breath. No more incessant death-rattle. No more eternal hiss. Awkward moisture gathered in his eyes. It sat, surface tension taut, but didn't spill over. Like he'd lost a limb but didn't know it yet.

He thought of his father. An efficient and studious worker who filed papers in a paper filing facility until his death some years prior. The Man With No Tears didn't know about eye moisture then, unsure of what that would be or how it might feel. The accumulated walls of grief crashed down around him, revealing the empty husk waiting inside. He could see himself as he truly was. Washed out, smog-bleached, vacant, a sad cartoon vignette in a tattered suit and tie, cradling a cat encased in tar. A cat encased in tar, now silent.

The Man With No Tears' failures were plain to see. He'd been a shit son, a shit neighbor, a shit employee, a shit citizen, a shit lover, a shit friend, and a shit pet owner. He'd barely gotten around to being shit at several other things, too. More forgotten futures now lamented. More lives abandoned before they'd been considered.

Water sitting in his eyes, he allowed himself to be pulled into the derelict building. Glass cracked under his feet, a shard slicing into his brutalized toe, but he couldn't feel it above the bizarre chorus. Still holding brick cat to his face, he pleaded with it to come back. His new hum breathed across its mouth-opening, and he waited for it to match his new song. But it remained silent, unmoving.

The air around him was thick with atmosphere. Not smog, not soot dust, not smoke. Cool air. He breathed into brick cat's mouth, begging and begging. Nothing.

Deeper into the building new sounds emerged. In the shadows figures shifted. Spindly eldritch arms stretched out toward The Man With No Tears. He hummed into brick cat's mouth, unable to be afraid. Unable to be anything. But somehow, for the first time maybe, able to be something.

The leather of his shoes squeaked on the filthy concrete until he was standing on something else. Something soft and warm. Inviting, even. But then it grabbed him.

A wood-covered rope, wrapping itself around his ankle and pulling him down. In the struggle, he dropped brick cat, sending it clattering across the strange floor. He let out a yelp, scrambling to free himself from the wooden noose that had pulled seductively taut against his leg. The strain was pleasant and unleashed a new sensation. One not unlike the acid on his toe. Sensual. But there was no time to embrace it.

He pulled himself free and grabbed brick cat. The impact on the floor had created a hairline crack on the surface of the tar and The Man With No Tears feared the worst. First he tried to rub the crack away, to seal it, but nothing came of it. Then he noticed the bud. On the brick cat's back sprouted a small brown pullulate. It was something most folks might miss, or even ignore, but it held a profound weight for him.

I can't believe I broke my pet... he said to himself, the moisture threatening to escape the prison of his eyelid. Between the lack of a hiss, the fracture, and this new parasite, he was sure the beast was gone. He placed brick cat to his face, humming at it one last time, as if to comfort it.

It hissed back.

Its breath was something different. An angular, unnatural

cadence. One that matched his new hum, which in turn matched the strange rhythm emanating throughout the building. Overjoyed, The Man With No Tears held brick cat to his chest, thanking it over and over for being there. The sprouting bud chafed against his torso as another figure shifted behind him.

Turning to look, he saw row after row of barren trees. They sprouted out of the concrete, crumbling it as they subtly moved. Their roots bled through the surface like veins beneath skin, pulsing and shifting in abstract patterns. Hair raised on the back of The Man No Tears' neck as they swayed together. The song in the warehouse growing louder and sharper. It flowed with their movements. It flowed through them, and into him.

The sprout became hard, sharp, threatening to pierce through his chest. Pulling brick cat into view, it had become a short stick with tines shooting off in various directions. In front of his eyes it grew and grew, until it was too big to hold comfortably. Dropping it to the ground, the song went quiet; the room silent but for The Man With No Tears' hum, brick cat's hiss, and the pervasive echo of distant dripping water into a puddle.

A crack broke the relative quiet, as the freshly formed fallow tree burst free from the tar and slowly crawled towards the rest of its flock. Brick cat was in roughly connected pieces, its hiss dulled. Scooping the poor creature up, The Man With No Tears brought his pet to his mouth and kissed it. Tar crumbled on his chapped lips. And it still hissed. And he still hummed. And the song still echoed through the dilapidated building. But the hiss was waning. It limped along, quieter and quieter with each second until it ran into silence.

Brick cat was loose in his arms. Lifeless. Flexible in a way it hadn't ever been. He wondered what its life was like before it came into his. He wondered if it was content with their time together. If it was scared to go silent. To fully die.

Outside the warehouse, the sprawling grey dinge of the world pressed on, as it always had. The distant drum droned overhead, the clanging of pistons and grinding of gears and clacking of levers invaded the lives and minds and souls of the population. It bore into them and replaced their hopes and dreams with sludge and grit and dirt and fetid pools of shimmering iridescence. The thing it had always done. The black planet soared above them, both in orbit and out, both material and not. A woman inside answered calls, directing them elsewhere via a giant switchboard. The clicking of jack plugs sliding into ports filling the small room. A black, faceless clock hung on the wall above her, its ticking ringing out across the skies of both worlds.

But inside that warehouse, with the song and the hum and the silent hiss and the trees and the rust and the rubble and the milky blood and the terror and the frenzy and the numb and the silence of never being quiet and the forgotten futures and the haunting memories, The Man With No Tears let a single line of water drip out of his eyelid and scroll down his cheek. It landed on his limp pet who sat in the silence of death.

As the trees shivered around him, their roots embracing the smaller stick as one of their own, their collective song coming to a crescendo, The Man With No Tears held his pet in watery-eyed silence before gently placing it on the ground —it's final resting place—and walking into the vibrating thicket; allowing the trees to tangle his limbs in harsh wooden restraints which dug into his skin and pulled him under, into his final resting place.

FLESH CRUCIFIX

WE DIDN'T REALIZE JAMES WAS MISSING UNTIL HIS GIRLFRIEND, Gloria, stopped coming around. She was always there, pilfering our beer, eating our food, not cleaning up after herself. But one day the beer fridge was as stocked as it had been the night before and there weren't shattered bits of pita chips all over the couch or a pile of unwashed dishes in the sink.

The house was silent.

Rat told us she'd heard Gloria and James had been hanging out at a recently established punkhouse in Tangle-town. One none of us had ever seen flyers for, much less heard anyone talk about. Rat said they were freegans or something. Sounded like a bunch of inconsequential noise to me.

Fuckin' Rick suggested that maybe she had just gone home for a minute, but Rat called that bullshit right away. She never went home. In fact, we weren't even sure if she had a home. Like one day James just let her in and she just suddenly lived with us without so much as a conversation. Or paying for rent. Or contributing to the beer fridge. Or buying her own fucking food.

I wouldn't have even been mad about it if she had thrown in, or simply taken from James' share. I worked long and thankless shifts at The Triangle Natural Foods Co-op to afford that sourdough bread and bargain bin minestrone and vegetable soup, keeping myself alive with the vegetarian essentials. And I stole my share of the fridge beer from the loading dock of corporate liquor store on the other side of town fair and square. It was the principal of the matter.

With her gone, we figured we'd see James at some point. Like he might crawl out of that cave that was his attic bedroom and seek sunlight, or at least a piss and some Hamm's. Perhaps he'd lumber down from his room, days long hangover in his watery eyes and listen to Killing Joke and Amebix records with me until we passed out, like we had so many other nights. But the longer he didn't come out, the more it slipped my mind. Like a water spot on basement wall that eventually grows into a full-blown black mold situation. Not that I know about that or anything.

Rat was the first to bring it up. She came home one night after a late bartending shift at The Anchor, a favorite dive for punks and other assorted miscreants. She slammed down on the couch next to me, kicking off her leather boots with a clunk--breaking me from my haze of almost sleep. Rat's VHS of Lair of the White Worm was playing on our shitty tube tv —a gift from the dumpster gods the previous spring when all the college kids abandoned their dorms.

She let out a heavy sigh and grabbed my last room-warmed beer from the table in front of me before gulping it down in a single—albeit overlong—swig.

"Do you think James is dead?" is all she said.

Panic put a knife to my heart. *Wait, is that possible* I thought to myself, but also apparently out loud.

"The fuck do you mean?" She threw the can over her shoulder, to the unknown cavern between the couch and the wall; a place we never go.

"I don't fucking know, wouldn't it like smell or something?" I tried to understand what it would even look like for us if he had died. Rent was due in a few days. Money was lean. Times were tight. Food costs rising. Beer ever trickier to pilfer. "I think we'd notice it…" I trailed off, hoping; staring off into the middle distance between the tv and dusty record shelf. I kept hearing James' voice in my head from the last time we hung out. "I gotta get my shit together…"

"Guy is worthless anyhow. I guess it wouldn't matter." She got up and disappeared behind the door to her bedroom with a soft thud. The low drone of Baroness' First fired up almost immediately.

The question of what was going on beyond the door at the end of the hall itched like a fresh wound as Lady Marsh serpentined across the warbling screen. I was out cold before she was done. Boots still on, warm beer nestled between my thighs.

A door slammed shut and I awoke to razors of light cutting across my vision. The tv ran a loop of silent static. I got up and walked through my pile of discarded Hamm's cans to take a piss and hop in the shower, hoping to wash some of the slept-in filth and beer sweat off. A smell that lingered on the couch long after I was done.

In the bathroom I thought I heard a noise above me. Past the ceiling and the joists and the subflooring was James' room. Not talking or humming or even moaning, though lord knows I heard enough of that from our time together, but something soft and wet. A squelching.

It turned my stomach, so I cranked the shower and hopped in, washing off days of stale human stench and grime. The summer had turned hellish, and near daily bike rides to and from the co-op had me hemorrhaging sweat.

By the time I was done and had stumbled into my room, I'd pushed the sounds from my mind. After throwing my damp clothes into the festering void of my closet, a dark cool met me as I fell nearly naked into bed with the fan circling above. Subtle wisps of dust danced off my record and book-shelves in the low light and the pleasant, rhythmic song of show flyers and band posters rattling against plaster walls in the smooth airflow brough a sense of relaxation and normalcy.

I wished I hadn't stopped smoking, opting instead to put on Requiem's Storm Heaven LP. My day slowly melted away as I switched record after record after record. Never getting dressed. Never turning the lights on. No plans. No responsibilities. Just me, the bed, the fan, and the music. Surrounded by my meager book and record collection. A perfect day off.

Until I heard someone walking through the living room.

Everyone was supposed to be at work, or at least that's what I thought. Of course, any of them could have been cut early or came home sick or to attend some personal business I wasn't privy to. But it felt different than that. The sensation of another person just beyond my bedroom door was strangely unfamiliar. Alien and uncomfortable. Like an intrusion.

My heart throbbed in my throat, and I didn't know why, but I threw on some pants and a shirt before opening my door as quietly as I could. The fucking thing squeaked the moment I started to pull.

A lean figure stood in my living room, staring away from me, unresponsive to the noise my door had made. They were cast in backlight so I couldn't make out anything specific aside from their slender frame as they gently shifted amongst the empty cans beside the couch.

I looked around, trying to find out if they were alone, or even how they got in before clearing my throat saying *can I help you?*

They didn't respond. As I took a step out of my room, I glanced down the hall. Subtle light shimmered off the scattered thrift store art hanging on the walls.

The door to James' room was open. A foul stench suddenly met my nose, and I gagged, hard, my core threatening to convulse. Tears streamed down my cheeks as she turned and met my eyes.

Gloria, I muttered, half to myself.

But she was all wrong. Gaunt with thick veins bulging under her sallow flesh. Her eyes were deeply sunken into her skull. Fingers broken and gnarled, dripping dark fluid. She tried to speak, but all that slipped past her mottled teeth was a dull croak.

The front door swung open and before I had a chance to react Gloria was gone, the door to James' room slamming behind her just as Rat stumbled in with a bombastic laugh, her arms overloaded with grocery bags. Fuckin' Rick was right behind her.

"The fuck you doing, dude?" Fuckin' Rick practically spat on me as he spoke, passing by me with a case of beer. "Everything OK?"

I stood there in silent disbelief, unsure of what I had seen. Unsure if it was even real. The baffled look on my face was only met with more questions as Rat returned from the kitchen, handing me a High Life. "Whoa! What's going on, guy?"

We walked as a procession to the couches, and I sat before I spoke, taking a long pull from the Deer Brand Rat had given me. I wished I had a cigarette.

"Gloria…she's here. But like, not ok…"

They met each other's eyes but didn't say anything.

"She was just standing here, ran like a fucking rabbit back up the stairs as y'all were opening the door. Scared the shit outta me. But like, she's also not ok. Or. I don't know, she looked fucking sick or something. I think she needs our help…"

"Wait, is James with her?" Fuckin' Rick said, eyes fixed on the ceiling above.

"Not ok how?" Rat said, taking a swig of beer. "Do we need to call someone? Is it injury? Contagion? Is she fucked up on drugs or some shit? You gotta give us more than 'she's not ok,' shit, dude."

"I don't know…but I think we should go up there…" As I glanced down the hall at the door, a skeletal hand reached down my throat, gripping my heart.

Rat was the first down the hall, tossing her battle vest into her room as she walked by the open doorframe. She gently knocked and we stood in silence, listening only to the pounding of blood in our ears. "Fuck this," Fuckin' Rick said, doing a full-on cop-knock with the bottom of his tightly closed fist.

The impact echoed up the wooden staircase and we waited again. Breath on hold, necks strained for better listening above us. There was something scratched along the ceiling and Fuckin' Rick jumped, beer splashing all over us, the walls, and the floor.

I wanted to laugh, but I could barely breathe. The anxiety was welling in my chest and without thinking I grabbed the doorknob and twisted, pulling the door open.

The rank odor hit first. A sickly tumorous smell mixed with death scents both animal fresh and sweetly lingering. We all gagged. I held my breath and started to head up the stairs, but Rat grabbed my arm. "You sure? Shouldn't we just, like, call someone or something?"

"Who the fuck are we gonna call, Rat? The fucking cops?" Fuckin' Rick said, mockingly while directing our eyes down to my ACAB knuckle tattoos.

"Obviously not, but I don't know, like a health crisis line or something. Shits fucked…" She trailed off, her grip easing on my arm. I started walking, her fingers sliding away gently as she stayed firmly in place. Fuckin' Rick didn't follow either. They both murmured when I got to the turn on the stairs and drifted out of sight.

It was dark at the top of the stairs and Rat calling my name almost gave me a heart attack. *Jesus*, I whispered under my breath. It took a moment for my eyes to adjust, as the windows were all covered by heavy blankets. Rat called again, and I yelled back, "Either come up here with me or shut the fuck up."

Her boots were heavy on the stairs, stopping about halfway up at the turn. I looked back at her and she was suddenly so much smaller than she lived in my mind. Not the tall, intimidating metalpunk I met at a party all those years ago whose easy laugh and big smile immediately disarmed you, but rather a miniature version of herself, hiding an obvious tremble in her voice like a child scared of a sleepover ghost story but putting on a brave face. "Look…"

He was in front of us, off at the other end of the room. Next to the brick wall that ran through the whole building and was once attached to a fireplace many years ago. A shadow. Arms outstretched.

I fumbled on the nearest wall for a light switch, but I didn't know the attic space well enough, so it was based on nothing but hope.

Something shifted in the darkness and the world slowed to a halt for a moment. Just Gloria and I and nothing else. She pulled herself along the unfinished floorboards. I imagined a gathering army of sharp splinters digging into her leg and hip.

Her eyes stared into me, and she was silently mouthing something, but I couldn't make out what it was; just mechanical movement in the darkness. It reminded me of being alive.

Rat didn't seem to notice and ran past me, toward the figure by the brick wall. She was screaming. It echoed in the rafters of the unfinished room, but it didn't register to me as much at all. Gloria's eyes, glistening in the darkness. Her mouth moving over and over and over were all I could focus on.

Rat pulled one of the blankets off the window with a crash as the heavy fabric got tangled in James' drum set. With the decay of a cymbal, the evening light broke into the darkness, and I was suddenly aware that Gloria wasn't trying to communicate anything.

She was eating jagged bits of flesh torn from her own legs and arms alongside that of stinking fur-covered animals and disembodied limbs. Her blood-caked mouth struggled against the tough meat, and she chewed and chewed and chewed with a squelching that echoed in my ears long after it had gone silent.

Then the room was filled with a panicked wail, and I broke my shared gaze with Gloria. Scanning the attic full of various animal carcasses and remnants of dead human bodies that would never be whole again, there was James kneeling by the brick wall, the flesh from his back flayed and missing. Angry raw muscle, dripping fat, and shimmering bone fell off him in clumps; greasy, rotting masses that littered the floor around him like a magic circle.

His hands were clasped together in prayer and his lidless eyes were staring up at the wall. I ran over to him, grabbing the open muscle of his arm, face covered in tears, but he wouldn't move. He just stared up at the wall, eyes fixed. Small flaps of skin where his lids had been occasionally dancing in phantom blinks. His breathing was pained. Labored.

I followed his gaze to the wall.

Above us hung a large cross made of flesh, muscle, tendon, nerve, bone, fur, feather, cartilage, organs, and hair. It shimmered. It glowed. It called out to me.

The flesh pulsed and writhed with life, but also dripped rotting amniotic fluid. Both alive and dead. Both living and inanimate. Both sentient and oblivious.

Rat kneeled next to us, tears pouring from her reddened face. They met mine on the floor, next to all the rancid chunks of James and other bits—both animal and human.

The cross held no anger, no rage, no sorrow, no judgment. It held only death. There were no more questions in my mind, there was only flesh and death. Rot and acceptance. Entropy which will and power and greed and love and every-thing else held no sway over.

It was pure. It was final.

The crucifix, or something *inside* the crucifix, wormed into my brain and unlocked memories older than words. Older than thoughts conveyed through words. I was brought back to a state before symbols and their understanding. To a place of pure flesh.

Flesh free of intellectual domestication. Flesh free of psychological chains. Flesh felt wholly in itself. As it is, not as we think it is. Beyond thoughts. Pure animal existence.

Eventually Fuckin' Rick met us in prayer. I don't recall when, but at some point the room filled with shrieking and pounding and then he collapsed next to me, his hands dripping in blood which too met our tears and blood and fetid meat on the floor around us, growing our magic circle.

My legs grew numb and then were overcome with pain and then numb again. It went on like this for a while, but I paid it no mind. There was just us and the inevitable. These bodies mere tombs. These lives worth spent only in prayer.

In sacrifice.

In the gratitude and grace of the knowledge of death. Of rot.

In worship to the crucifix of flesh.

We scratched and clawed at our bodies, then at each other's. Some parts for consuming so we would stay alive, but others were for the sacrament. Parts of all of us, bones, gristle, fat, flesh, muscle, hair, and teeth met in a cacophony of pieces of the dead who surrounded us. Feather and fur and beak and claw and nail and arm and tattooed skin.

A long distant part of me watched in abject terror, but it was so small and quiet that it scarcely registered. My old life was dying, and in its place grew something beautiful.

Before long we were done and collectively weeping at what sat before us: another cross. This one truly ours.

Blood pooled beneath us, and my limbs were well past weak and into atrophy, but I forced myself upward, stumbling on my feet like a cartoon baby deer. My muscles screamed. My bones creaked I paid them no mind. The rest followed and we gathered up our cross, heading out of the attic, through our front door, and out of the building. Hoping to share the good news with anyone who would hear it.

JIZZ CHRIST

Half elated and half exhausted, Spencer placed the bottle of murky liquid onto the rickety table in the center of his claustrophobic art studio. His knees trembled, pulling him to the wooden floor. He fought against the dizziness, focusing on the task at hand. Lighting a candle, he raised a stick of red wax and dropped it into a small brass bowl. With his other hand, he secured the cork top in the mouth of the bottle, finalizing months of work. A thin stream of fluid dripped between his legs onto the ground. In the dim twilight, dirty wood shimmered momentarily through the pearlescent dollop before hissing and bubbling. An acrid aroma wafted up from the drop, one of burnt hair and sour disinfectant.

The candle fit snugly into a chamber beneath the bowl, melting the wax stick. Inhaling the vapors, Spencer saw stars for a moment, but that too passed. He slowed his heavy breathing, placing the top of the bottle into the melted wax, sealing it, careful not to leave it too long for fear the glass would crack.

The bottle was something a hipster whiskey company would sell their poorly made booze in; shaped like the first third of a horseshoe, curved perfectly to fit next to a thigh. About nine inches tall and four wide, the glass was worn, aged. When empty, light cascading through it revealed uneven surfacing; imperfect bubbled glass. It was handmade. Antique.

As he turned and shifted the now full vessel, metal clinked against the inside. The bottle had been his grandmother's. The thought gave him pause. Not exactly discomfort. Something approaching it.

If your transgression isn't personal, what's the point?

Cooling wax slowly dripped down the side of the short neck and onto his thumb as Spencer stared into the final result of months of work. Through the fluid, the antique crucifix was already starting to patina. The savior's face eroded. Shimmering gold flaked away to expose the pitted lead underneath. The cross too was a family heirloom. This one from his father's side.

It had hung over his grandfather's bed throughout the man's childhood and then his father's, and when Spencer was born it hung over his. At least until he took it down at fourteen, throwing it into a trash can behind their garage. Within a week it was back up, and he threw it out again. This cold war lasted months, until he'd finally had enough. Instead of throwing it away or hiding it somewhere in basement storage, Spencer tucked it between his box spring and mattress, right next to tattered issues of Manual, Bi-Sex, and the much more easily accessible Penthouse.

The cross sat adjacent to his meager porn collection and a bottle of lotion for years. Just another reminder that he was broken. Just another reminder that something within him was beyond redemption.

His father never asked about the cross. If he found it, the hiding place in proximity to porn was too terrible for him to bring up. Beyond punishment, his parents weren't much for talking, especially about anything uncomfortable, so the silence was expected. Their discomfort and reserve were reliable at the very least. And at fourteen, Spencer was past the days of conversations regarding mysterious holes seared in his sheets and underwear. Those had been agony.

Their assertion that he'd purposefully burned away the

resultant stains from his fits of disgusting self-abuse, just to hide them, as though they wouldn't have noticed. Their judgment was that he was an idiot. A monster. A pervert.

And he felt like one. For his desires, for his lust, for his loneliness. But also for the way his body was born monstrous, unnatural. He was rotten from the inside. Wrong. Broken. Forged with grotesque parts.

As the cross corroded in the bottle, he heard his mother's pained crying, his father's heated voice. Someone at church had caught him kissing a boy behind the maintenance shed one hot summer day. Or maybe he was misremembering the inciting incident. There had been so many, despite his parents warning that the fires of lust burned in the flesh no different than the fires of hell. Spencer couldn't help it, didn't want to either. If it wasn't that boy, it was certainly another or a maybe girl. Those infractions always caught less heat.

He could always see the hope in his father's eyes when it was a girl. Like maybe he wasn't so far beyond the pale. Maybe he was actually salvageable. Not beyond redemption. Not irreparably damaged. Not too far gone. Fixable. Human.

But that look never lasted long before it gave way to cold disgust. Spencer moved out when he was sixteen; crashed on couches, slept on floors, talked his way into beds at homeless shelters. Anything to be out of that house. Everything he owned was inside a backpack and locked in a steamer trunk that had been at the edge of his bed since he was a little kid.

And that's where he found the crucifix, all those years later. He'd come across it one day while trying to find a picture of his parents for an art project he was doing. The photo never materialized, but finding the cross left him to abandon that idea and start something new. Something personal and uncomfortable; something more challenging.

It had taken him ages to figure out how to get the cross into the bottle. Multiple attempts at rigging the arms to go down and pop back up once they were beyond the short neck. First came cutting them off, though reattaching them was the issue. He was not an engineer, but eventually, he settled on some springs rigged inside makeshift housings on the back. The arms were reattached with small, gold-plated hinges, matching the shiny finish. It did the trick. He hoped it would hold.

The first time he got it in, he was terrified it might break. That he wouldn't be able to get it back out if something went wrong. But it fit perfectly. Once it was secure, he began the real work.

He filled the bottle with all the poison he'd been taught to hold inside over the years.

Spencer stared at the culmination of his efforts and felt nothing. Not catharsis or excitement. Not exhaustion or elation. Simply nothing. Something so close, so goddamn personal, and yet it was just another addition to the yawning pit in his stomach.

They say art is a salve, but perhaps it's also a burden.

NATHAN WASN'T sure what he had walked into. The small art gallery was that in name only. More a couple of adjoining rooms with desks and bookshelves crammed into various corners, and art hastily hung up on walls or precariously balanced on poorly constructed wooden pillars littered throughout the space. The lighting was essentially office industrial rather than museum. Ramshackle and spliced together with concern only for utility. He wondered how many errant holes in the plaster the paintings obscured.

While it wasn't a packed house, there were a lot of people wandering around looking at art, most with BYOB cheap beers or economical bottles of wine in hand. He looked for Monica, Sandy, and Eric through a scattered assortment of punks in black denim vests covered by illegible band logos, hipster grad students, weirdo artists, concerned friends who'd been cajoled into coming along, and the odd journalist or two—the latter of whom most likely swindled local alt-weekly papers into paying them to do write-ups for the show. She was nowhere to be found.

The Bell Tower had been a staple of the DIY art and music scene for several years, giving the art a specific air of unspoiled and secret credibility; underground, even. None of these artists had pieces in any of the prominent, more corporately-funded galleries, and it was unlikely any of them were going to be in museums one day. But that wasn't a reflection on the quality of the art. Much of it was mesmerizing. All of it unique. Though you'd have to forgive a piece or two that felt more at home in a high school art show than a carefully curated exhibit.

As Nathan walked around, studying each piece, he took special care to read titles and artist statements, seeing references to older artistic movements, philosophy, obscure films and literature, and personal trauma. The last one made the most sense, given that it was the theme of the show. Political and personal symbolism intertwined, some overtly, some over the top, but others much more subtly. A few pieces were captivating in their statements. A couple were cartoonishly simple takes on complex issues.

An elemental scent caught his nose before he saw it. In a corner on a pillar an unassuming bell jar atop a dark wooden plate. An old glass hip-flask full of thick pearly liquid. A graying, mottled crucifix scarcely visible suspended inside. On the walls surrounding the piece hung used bedsheets with splotchy, irregular holes. They were draped like the dossal curtains of an old church altar.

The placard simply said, "Jizz Christ."

Nathan almost laughed, but instead he stared at it, taking it in. Wondering what it was. What the artist intended. Certainly a reference to Andres Serrano's famed, controversial photograph, but through the lens of appropriative art. To Nathan, it sat somewhere between contempt for the history of art and a dumb joke. Subversive but ultimately silly and childish. He'd seen a lot of that at college. And yet, there was something else to it. Something toiling away beneath. It wormed inside him.

The interplay between the holes in the sheets and the tarnished, barely visible surface of the crucifix. He couldn't put it into words or meaning, but it evoked a stirring in him; sensations familiar and primal on a molecular level. Memories too repulsively personal. Not the revulsion of unwanted bodily fluids or harsh lighting on broken flesh. No. The revulsion of bearing witness to a profane—or perhaps sacred—intimate act.

As his mind wandered, the elemental scent again gripped him with intimations both familiar and foreign. Haunting. Secret. His cheeks flushed red as he recognized the smell of vaguely singed fabric and burnt hair. There was something else beneath, something new and unique. A different flavor.

Heart pounding in his throat, he was hit with a barrage of conflicting emotions and sensations. Memories. Trauma. Excitement.

At 14, making out with a girl at a friend's party. Forced into a closet together while everyone waited on the other side laughing and cheering. Awkward glances, his hesitation. Not sure if he liked girls. Not sure if he liked boys, but he thought he might. Maybe both. A sense of elation, fear, and anticipation. The way she leaned in, as if to comfort but also to get what she was seeking. The taste of her lips. The brief sweetness that etched into his tongue before her sudden shift in demeanor. Her panic. Her pain. The blisters that sprouted so abruptly on her lips and tongue. Wailing as she ran out of the room.

Parental voices. "Chemical burn." "A freak accident." "Unexplainable." His tears, silenced. Alone. Not just that night, but from then on.

Nathan was made a monster by the other kids. They abandoned him—shunned him—for burning her face. He didn't even know what he'd done; much less how he'd done it. Nor why they scorned him so harshly.

His parents took him to a doctor, old and gray, who said

everything was fine. But Nathan watched the wooden stick the doctor placed on his tongue burn away as it was discarded into the trash. No one else seemed to notice.

Despite a clean bill of health, his parents never stopped with the questions, with the knowing glances at each other; steeping in their discomfort. His mother routinely asked him why he kept tearing up his socks and underwear. But he couldn't control it, and they wouldn't listen.

As he got older, he withdrew. Not just from them but from everyone—not that there were many friends by that point anyhow. At least until a new kid, Tanner, came to school. He was different; kind and quiet. By this time Nathan knew what he liked, and Tanner fit perfectly. They struck up an easy friendship, one with awkward hugs and overlong eye contact. By the end of the summer, they were maybe an item. It was never said expressly, and certainly not discussed with others. A silent merging of hands done only in unlit places.

Nathan was never sure how to broach the topic of kissing or sex, so he just didn't. Anytime Tanner tried, Nathan firmly declined. Not because he didn't want to, but so he wouldn't hurt him. He never knew how to put it into words. Tanner carried the rejection and sadness, but never pushed the issue. Nathan wondered what Tanner thought. Maybe Nathan was too in the closet to be comfortable, but even back then in a small town, that wasn't a term either of them had ever really heard.

Assuming Tanner would eventually lose his patience, Nathan tried to not overthink it. At least until he caught him making out with a girl in the library. As Nathan ran to the bathroom, tears burned small holes in his favorite shirt. Onlookers laughed as he passed them. Just another damaged queer in love with a boy.

After that, Nathan avoided Tanner until he showed up one night at Nathan's house, unannounced, drunk, and angry. He was pushy, harshly asking why Nathan hadn't returned his calls, wondering why he'd been so afraid, so frigid. In the midst of ranting, Tanner forced their lips together, his stinking breath crawling down Nathan's throat, turning his stomach. But the embrace didn't last long.

Tanner's screams were deafening. The moment he'd forced himself onto Nathan, Nathan spat in his mouth. It dribbled down his chin, leaving ugly blisters on raw, reddened skin. A new part of Nathan awoke at that moment, as he looked into Tanner's bloodshot eyes and saw shock coiled with fear.

No one came to Tanner's panicked aid, nor Nathan's. And the neighborhood stayed silent as Tanner ran back to his car and drove away, muttering and crying as his taillights disappeared into the darkness.

In the gallery, the smell was so familiar. Nathan knew it too well. Years of research in books on medical anomalies and rabbit holes down the strangest corners of the internet brought him nothing. He assumed he was the only one. And he feared talking with doctors about it, feared they would put him in a lab to be studied or lock him up for being potentially dangerous. Not quite human. Abnormal. Grotesque.

That lingering, personal smell. There was something else now. He wasn't alone in his deviation. He wasn't fucking alone.

Searching through the gallery, he asked several strangers if they knew who'd created the piece. No one could tell him. It was the only one left unattributed. Doggedly, he made his way to the back of the building, through a heavy black door he'd spotted several people go in and out of. Past that was a long dirty hallway with more unmarked doors along the left side and a set of stairs at the end.

He tried one. It was locked. The next opened onto a pair of surprised occupants who stared at him blankly. The room was a tiny art studio and the couple were cutting lines of white powder with a torn piece of cardstock. As quickly as he opened it, he closed it. A mixture of embarrassment and laughter rose up inside of him, matching the reaction he heard from the other side of the door once it clicked shut.

From the stairwell came clanging and the whine of a few

stringed instruments being tuned. All of it was scarcely audible, overpowered by the indistinct chatter of an anxious crowd.

Nathan pursued the sound down the stairs and nestled himself within a group of onlookers as a band finished setting up and broke into their first song. Haunting waves of gothic folk music filled the small room. Something like old-time labor songs, spirituals, and murder ballads by way of Bauhaus and Swans. Monica waved to him from within the throng, but he pushed her from his mind. He'd caught the scent.

From across the room, Nathan thought he spotted the source. At first, he wasn't sure, but the moment they locked eyes he could taste it. An irreal and bizarre sensation of recognition, of knowing. He trusted his gut. He trusted the pheromones.

Through the congregation, he maneuvered his way over to the stranger, who hovered half-obscured by dim lighting at the edge of the crowd on the far end of the makeshift stage—less an elevated platform and more simply a spot on the ground where the band was playing. As soon as Nathan got close enough, he leaned in and shout-whispered in the stranger's ear, "I love your piece. Jizz Christ, right?"

Without missing a beat, Spencer faced him and smiled crookedly, "How the hell do you know? Do we know each other?"

Nearly shouting, "No, but this is gonna sound crazy. I know you. I mean, I *know* you. What you are. We're the… we're the same…"

Nathan's words haunted the space between them and Spencer's demeanor immediately changed. What had been a smile became a glare as he pushed past Nathan and the audience to reach the solitary exit. Nathan followed as closely as he could, catching the tail end of his path through the crowd as it congealed back to one mass. Once they were both at the top of the stairs Spencer turned back towards him. "Look, don't fuck with me, and don't follow me. I don't know you, and whatever this weird bullshit is, I don't want anything to do with it."

He turned to go, but Nathan grabbed his hand, "Please. I'm not trying to fuck with you. Just listen to me. I'm like you. I mean, we're *fucking* the same. The smell. I know it. I have it. The—I don't know, I've never put it into words before—the acidic nature of my body. It's like yours. I recognize the burn holes in the sheets. I've done that too. All the goddamn trauma. The—fuck, I don't know—aberrant nature of just existing. You're here. I'm here. We are the fucking same."

A single tear rolled down Nathan's cheek, searing a hole in his shirt.

Reluctantly at first, Spencer squeezed Nathan's hand, only then aware that they were still clasped onto each other. Tears of his own rolled through his beard, dripping off his chin, burning holes in the trampled, dusty carpet below them.

ALL THE GOLD FLAKED AWAY, the crucifix had dissolved into an uneven pair of intertwined sticks with a lumpy, inhuman figure attached, and the once pearlescent liquid had both yellowed and grayed with time. Jizz Christ sat in the corner of the mixed-use art space for a few weeks, as each of the artists hoped for a buyer or art dealer to contact them. A freshly rancid smell permeated the carpet and walls nearest to the podium, but it was elusive and fleeting.

Spencer watched himself soften and open up to the idea of discussing what his life had been like. Something about how Nathan carried himself—this uneven mix of self-assured awkward—made Spencer want to talk about it, even the things he'd long-ago promised himself he'd never tell anyone.

There was so much pain and isolation, and at points, he thought it was going to drive him mad. The paranoia about anyone finding out, not just on a social level, but for his own safety that someone might come for him or that he would be forced into a cage. Life was always a giant, scary unknown, but a part of him wished other people could see that there were layers to that idea. For some, it was a scarier, greater unknown.

Verbalizing these feelings and thoughts as he looked into Nathan's eyes, he felt comfort and safety for the first time. He was wholly heard and understood. No longer stuck in the shadows, no longer self-relegated to the sidelines. And that was more frightening than anything else he could have imagined.

"When I was a kid at church, I learned about this missionary in the–I don't know–the '30s or something. It doesn't matter. There were a few grainy photos and one super old piece of film that was simply him walking up the side of a steep hill in the snow.

"His whole thing was that he'd gone from America to someplace like Siberia–I'm not sure now, it was so fucking long ago–anyhow, he traveled to this distant country to ya know 'spread the word of God' or whatever bullshit they wanted to hide their colonialism behind.

"So dude ends up in these mountainous regions trying to sell his god to the indigenous folks of the Urals or wherever. His story was meant to be one of passion for Christ. One of solid, unmovable faith. But in the story, he never converts anyone. Not a single person. Heralded as some saintly figure for his resolve and commitment to the Lord.

"But really a life full of bitter disappointment and loneliness. Don't get me wrong, fuck him, and fuck that" Spencer coughed out a short laugh between words, "but my whole goddamn life, I couldn't help but feel partially the same. A stranger on an unknown mountain." Spencer paused, "This is too fucking weird…

"What I'm saying, is that for too long that's how I felt. How my life was. And now what? Not having that, not being alone in my misery and isolation. I guess I don't even know how to feel."

Nathan adjusted himself on the sofa and spoke, "Look, I

don't know. Lord trust me, I have no fucking idea. It's a game changer for me too if you haven't noticed. But, like, think about how different it could be. Fuck. How different already it is.

"Let me tell you a story. When I was in college, I tried to convince myself that it was all in my head. I'd had a bad experience with a boy in high school and, well, let's just say I ended up maiming him when he tried to force himself on me. But that trauma–that weird, so very individual pain and experience–I convinced myself, at least for a while there, that it was all in my head. No one else could verify who I was or what I went through. So maybe I was just crazy. I'd been studying abnormal psychology just to see if something I'd been experiencing was in the DSM5. What if I was broken in my mind, not my body?

"So I drank a bunch, like way more than I ever should, and went out to a party. There, with the help of a friend who knew I was lonely and perhaps a bit desperate, I met a guy. We keep drinking. Hands effortlessly grazing each other, lips moist, conversation charged. The whole deal. Which I should add seemed a bit of a miracle in Southern Illinois.

I take him back to my dorm room. We kiss. Hard. No screaming. So I work my way down and unzip his pants. Mind you, this is my first time touching a cock that isn't my own. He smells good, like cedar and lust. I put it in my mouth. Again, not really sure how to work it, but excited and willing. I'm going up and down, hand and mouth, but he's silent.

"It gets real slippery. Unnaturally so. Like I don't have enough saliva for this level of lubrication all these drinks later. Then it gets tacky like hardening syrup. I fumble for my bedside lamp.

"Blood. A lot of it. All over my hands. All over the sheets. All over his cock. Blood, and thin puddles of flesh. In terror, I look up at him. He's out cold. Probably passed out before my mouth ever even touched his then mangled dick. His lips, blistered and raw.

"Then comes the screaming, the onlookers, and eventually an ambulance.

"The same words I heard when I was a kid, "freak accident," "chemical burn," and a new one, "what did he take?" Pleading eyes, and no answers but my own weakness.

"Look, I don't know how to feel either. But I'm no longer alone. You're no longer alone. And that's worth something. If not for you right now in the chaos of this whole fucked up situation, maybe at the very least it's worth it to that kid you were, way back when. The one who was ashamed and afraid and made to feel subhuman…"

Spencer took a beat to process. He thought about the pain, the isolation. He thought about the blisters he'd left on the world. And maybe it could be different. But maybe they'd just be hurting each other. Before he could finish his thought, Nathan pulled him in, their tongues tightly entwined. Their lips locked together. Their beard hair coiled barbed wires.

And if there were blisters, if there was pain, perhaps–at the very least–Spencer thought, it would be of a brand new variety.

Nathan's hand trembled as he moved it down to Spencer's belt, clumsily unbuckling it. Spencer let out a small moan, filling the cavern their collective mouths had created. They tore at each other's shirts and pants, pausing their physical contact only when necessary to remove various clothes. An air of apprehension and excitement swallowed them both as they collided; all grasping hands and desperate cocks and twitching tongues and provoked thighs and warm, hungry mouths.

Flowing shadows of their rigid masculine forms burned onto the walls of the room, under sulfurous yellow light cascading from outside. For Nathan, it was dreamlike. As they writhed and thrust, he imagined them as two stags, bucking and clashing under a cold winter moon. Like Theseus slaying the Minotaur, locked in grasp now and forever. The very essence of self an illusion. The way Spencer tasted. His rugged hands grasping and caressing. Man in name only. Animal in essence and spirit.

Spencer breathed it all in. He allowed his restraints to loosen, and simply let go of the agony of isolation, the desperation for connection, touch, and a shared lust. All the days spent agonizing about being alone, about never again feeling someone near him, in him, in them. A single tear rolled off his cheek, burning a hole in the couch. Not the first, certainly not the last.

A shift came from inside. Something new, something wild. A call not felt for ages. He bored into Nathan; his eyes and his ass. Every screaming voice in his head went silent, clipping through his mind like the dead wax at the end of a record. Enveloped in warmth, in comfort, he let himself go.

No fear of damaging Nathan. No fear of damaging himself. Worst case scenario, their lust would destroy the world. Looking into Nathan's eyes, he reasoned that he was ok with that. After everything that had happened to him, happened to them both, maybe they could live with it.

In the empty gallery, his father's crucifix was reduced to nothing, and his grandmother's flask finally cracked under the acidic weight of his semen. As it ran down the pedestal, it left a trail of scorch marks. Burning through the dusty floor, what was left of Jizz Christ careened into the dark basement below.

PORTRAIT OF A RED TOWER

The photo hung in the corner of The Belltower, a mixed-use community space, for an art exhibit that weekend. Nothing fancy, and only mildly pretentious. A rag-tag group of local illustrators, screen printers, painters, sculptors, photographers, and mixed-media artists all showing off their work. The kinds of artists who don't get pieces in the big galleries on the other side of town, but also create genuine art, much of it probably deserving that grander fate it will never see.

Portrait of a Red Tower - Hank Chakowski the small piece of paper below the print read on one line, followed by *Analog Photograph on Gelatin Silver Paper* below it. An ominous tower loomed over a vast and desolate landscape. It was maybe three-stories tall, but somehow also appeared to pierce into the sky above. It also gave the impression that it was boring into the earth it stood upon, or perhaps trying to escape it. Yet, I don't know why I thought that. The longer I stared at it, the more intense the sensation was. And then I'd look away, return my gaze to the photograph, and the cycle would start again.

A pit grew in my guts. That was a familiar sensation, but I'd never had it from gazing at a photograph, much less one so innocuous as of a building and little else.

But not *nothing* else.

Don't get me wrong, there truly was nothing else in the photo, at least physically. But to say it was only a shot of a building would be to betray the entire thing. Obviously art is never just the thing it's showing. No. Not nothing else, just little else. The unease. The paranoia. The anxiety purchased by viewing the piece; that was the else.

I went home after the showing, happy to be free of forced social obligations and minor chatter with friends of friends. The only actual friend I had there was one of the artists, Katy, who was busy attending to everyone who wanted a piece of them. I understood, but was also annoyed.

That night after the art show, I poured myself a drink and listlessly scrolled social media on my phone. It pulled me in like a mindless dream: looking, closing one app, opening another, closing that *ad infinitum* until I was right back to the one I started with again and again and again.

On what was likely the seventh cycle, though it may as well have been the forty-fifth, an image grabbed my attention.

It was the tower.

A different photo of it. This one a night-time shot from a phone camera. Not low resolution, but minimal saturation, as the tiny lens struggled to pick up details in the low light. Though the tower also seemed to glow. Not literally, but it was like there was a phantom image of it behind itself, casting a strange aura around it.

I studied the picture, zooming in and out on various elements, trying to get a better look at everything. Just as in the portrait, the tower seemed to break endlessly into the sky, despite its meager stature. Unlike the portrait, this photo was at a strange angle, the ground tilting off to the side. Yet the building *almost* looked like it was standing in alignment with the perspective of the camera, like it had adjusted itself.

The longer I stared at it, the more I convinced myself this was true, but as with the photo in the gallery, once I looked away and came back to it, everything was normal again.

Wait. Not normal. Still ominous and strange, but not beyond the limits of the physical world as I had been seeing it.

Before I knew it, four full hours had passed. My back ached, my arms had begun to tremble in their static state for so long. Like the wind had been sucked out of me. I stiffly lumbered to my bedroom before I passed out, fully clothed and with my boots still on.

In the morning, I opened my phone to check my email. The tower stared back at me. Again, I combed through every section and area, trying to find some other landmark or indicator about where it was. Before I knew it, two hours had passed and I was late for work.

I ran to my car and drove as quickly as I could to the natural foods co-op. My boss was waiting for me in the front office, reprimand paperwork already filled out and simply awaiting my signature. I apologized and cooked up a bullshit story about my car getting a flat, but he didn't want to hear it and got me and my till onto the floor as quickly as possible, giving me stern eyes the whole time.

The day fizzled away around me and all I could think of was the red tower. Between customers, I caught myself sketching it out on a scrap of paper, getting every little detail right despite my typical drawings could only ever be called that in the most primitive of definitions.

Even from the drawing, the tower sent a shiver down my spine, like there was a menacing force inside, observing me. I wanted to crumple it up and throw it in the trash, but I couldn't. It stared into me until a waiting customer broke my gaze, startling me with a loud, "Is this lane open?"

I rang her groceries up, and the flurry of other customers that followed, occasionally glancing back down at the sketch that I couldn't flip over or discard or destroy, despite how it made me feel.

By the end of my shift I was exhausted so I stopped at the corner liquor store for a six-pack of Old Cat Beer and headed home, my mind swimming with little else but thoughts of the tower. Like it was calling out to me.

Once home, I grabbed my laptop and brought up the image. It stared through me. I taped the drawing I had made to the wall next to my couch so I could stare at that too. I did some reverse-image searches which mostly brought up aggregate sites picking from the spot I'd initially found it and several reposts on social media, most talking about how creepy the building was. But after pages and pages of those, I eventually found the origin point for it.

A long-abandoned message board with a post from 2005. It read:

Manitou81: spotted this weird ass building on my hike today creeped me out so I got a shot
eatshitb1rd: in town?
eatshitb1rd: or are you travellling again
THEETRAV: looks kinda gay
Peni420: lol
Peni420: but it is kewl
Manitou81: whatever.
Manitou81: yeah, here ain't been out in a minute

And then nothing else.

I searched Manitou81's name on the message board and combed through his posts and replies. There was nothing more related to the tower beyond the initial post. But that was also where his posts stopped. Digging through the board, it quickly grew vacant not long after.

His bio had a link to a personal website which was now up for grabs. Doing a google search of his name didn't bring much until eventually I found an old flickr account with the same handle.

The photos were mostly candid shots of friends partying and arty nature photos. And then there it was, staring back at me. The tower. No caption. The last photo he took. Like he had abandoned his digital life not long after posting it.

Combing through the images of friends, I started cross-referencing who also had them in their albums, eventually settling on the three names that popped up the most. I checked their accounts to see which was the most active. Two hadn't been touched in over a decade, but JijiGone had posted a photo a month prior. I sent her a message, hoping to hear back but not expecting anything. It read:

Jiji,

Sorry for the random message. This is weird and I know we don't know each other, but I'm interested in some more information about a photo your friend Manitou81 posted back in 2005. Is there any way you can give me his contact info or get me in touch with him? Sorry to bother you and thanks for your time.

I spent the rest of the night drinking my cheap beer and hunting for any other leads, but came up with nothing. Occasionally I would look over at the drawing of the tower or pull up the original photo on the laptop and just stare at it. It didn't make sense. I knew that rationally. Why this obsession with a photo of a building from almost 20 years ago?

But I also couldn't stop myself. It was so important to know, like the desire had been etched into my bones upon first glimpse of the damned thing.

Eventually the beer got to my head and I passed out, the tower watching me while I slept fitfully on my couch.

The next day was a day off from the co-op, so I got up and attended to some personal things, all the while the tower weighing on me. Like it was following me.

I saw it in the reflection of another building I passed while driving to the laundromat. Shimmering ominously behind me. When I turned my head there was nothing but a rundown gas station. I looked back and it was no longer in the reflection.

I got chills and started sweating heavily. I turned around and went home, where it was safe and comfortable, and nothing could watch me.

The cold air of my apartment was comfortable and calmed me down. Flipping open my laptop, I checked my email and found no reply from Jiji. I hunted again for more information about the photo but came up empty, so I went back to the source, remembering the photo from the art exhibit. *Hank Chakowski.* I searched his name and came up with little else than an architect in New York and a plumber in East End, Texas with a LinkedIn account.

Instagram, Twitter, and Facebook fared no better, only directing me to various accounts held by people who shared the name but didn't seem like photographers. And none were local.

I reached out to the email on the Belltower's website, asking if they had contact info for Chakowski, and that I had some questions about his work and then I waited.

I turned on my old printer and printed a copy of the photo Manitou81 had taken, taping it to my wall next to the sketch I had made. I stared at them. And they stared back at me.

Until I passed out.

In my dreams I was inside the red tower. Rusted machinery was squeaking and struggling, trying to run but unable to. I wandered the main floor, walking between these giant humming machines. The ground was slick with hydraulic fluid and fetid water, which trickled down a set of stairs at the end of the building.

When I reached them, I looked up and noticed elevated pathways far above the workfloor of the building and a ladder nearby leading up to them. Given the choice between down into the darkness below or up above to get a real scope of the place, I went up.

The ladder was slick with oil and gritty with old dirt, but I almost floated up to the top, setting my feet with unsettling ease onto the metal grating and gripping onto the side rails as firmly as I could. From that vantage, the building was impossibly large. It stretched out endlessly with nothing but the strange, broken machinery. There were no windows and no light fixtures, yet it was bright enough to see. Unnaturally lit.

I walked along the path until I couldn't walk anymore.

Nothing around me had changed except for slight variations among the machines. But the fluid on the floor was steadily rising. WIthin seconds it was over the tops of the machines and then oozing between the grating.

When it rose past my chin and I took my last breath, I woke up.

The towers on the walls were staring at me. The tower on my laptop was too. As was one on my phone.

I slammed my laptop shut just as a notification ding occurred, so I opened it back up to see an email from an organizer at the Belltower. They couldn't put me in touch with the artist as they were initially unaware of the piece. They found it on the wall and checked their records, realizing that it wasn't officially part of the show, and they had no idea who put it up.

I replied. *Can I have it?* And headed to the building before they responded.

The rising temperature outside had already crawled into my car, sending a wave of heat out the door when I opened it. The steering wheel was hot to the touch, so I tried to only use my fingertips.

As I made my way to the space, my phone buzzed in my pocket. Work.

I'd deal with it later. Getting written up again was no big deal, I was only a little late.

The Belltower wasn't technically open yet, but I could see them inside through a thin curtain on the door, so I knocked. After a moment someone opened the door and I told them who I was and how I had just talked to someone about the mysterious photograph.

The woman was confused, calling out into the building to see if anyone knew what I was doing there or what I was talking about. Another woman answered and came to the door, gesturing for me to come inside. The gallery room was still setup like it had been the night of my last visit, other than that the photograph was now taken down and in her hands.

She was in her mid-thirties and looked at me with a

puzzled expression. I told her about my email, and she told me she understood, but that I must not have gotten her response telling me that I probably couldn't have it.

I explained to her that I thought I had tracked down the artist, elaborating on the story of Manitou81, but saying he was the one who took this photo, and that I would get it back to him.

Initially, she scoffed, before shrugging her shoulders in a mix of defeat and indifference. She then handed me the framed photo. The attribution card was taped to the back.

She took the rest of my information just in case the artist returned asking about their work, making me promise I would give it back to them if that happened before I could get in contact with him, which I did.

And it wasn't a lie. While I didn't want to get rid of the photo now that it was in my possession, I also wanted to talk with the photographer more than anything.

I drove to work with another write-up waiting for me. Another set of scowling eyes from my manager. Another excuse about car troubles. And another wasted day ahead of me. In the time between ringing up customers, I kept catching myself smiling to myself about how lucky I had been to secure the photograph. Like a kid on Christmas morning with the special gift they'd wanted all year.

I probably looked like an idiot.

When my shift was over, I practically ran out the door and to my car. Once again I stopped for some Old Cat before heading home. Once there I cracked the first beer and studied my newfound prize.

Pulling some old pictures down from the wall, I hung it above the drawing and the printout. The way it gently glistened with the silver paper gave it a more menacing quality. With them all suspended next to each other, I wondered if they were even depicted the same side of the building.

Getting as close to each as possible, I studied every brick, every chip and crevasse. After two hours and all the beer, I was sure that they were from different sides of the building.

Which meant it was potentially desolate for what could have been miles around it.

My computer dinged and I opened it to check my email. It was Jiji.

Uhh, hi.

Yeah, that's pretty strange, and I wish I could help, but I'm guess I'm sorry to let you know that Manotau81 is dead. His name was Bradley. He died in 2005. I'm not sure what happened. Mental health stuff or drugs or something. By the time that happened we weren't really friends anymore. Sorry to be the bearer of bad news…

I closed the email. Crushed that I had come up with nothing but dead ends. With nothing left to do, I opened google maps, scouring outside of the city for dead end roads and desolate areas with a single building and nothing else. I looked until my eyes hurt.

It was getting late, but early enough that the liquor store was still open. I hopped in my car and drove over, grabbing a couple more six-packs of Old Cat and a fifth of Hornplow Whiskey Blend. Starting back in the direction of home, I decided that I would maybe have better luck driving to these areas and having a look myself.

I pulled up one on my browser history and set the phone's gps. The trip took longer than expected, not the 20 minutes I had hoped. It was forty-five minutes away, but I had the time so why not. After crossing several rivers, I ended up on a dark gravel road. There was a cluster of trees on one side, so my prospects didn't look good, but I kept going, hoping maybe they would open up and there would suddenly be nothing.

My cell signal got weak and the gps stopped working, but I kept going. Finding the place was the only thing on my mind and failure wasn't an option.

Eventually the road led to a chain link fence and several manufacturing buildings. They were clearly done for the day, so I pulled over, got out of the car, and screamed into the endless darkness above.

Kicking gravel I should have asked myself how I'd gotten there, why this mattered so much to me, but I didn't. I just stood under a single sulfur yellow bulb in the middle of nowhere and had a panic attack.

After it passed, I got back in my car, cracked a beer and drank it as quickly as possible. Then I headed home. Somehow the drive back felt longer than before, even after my cell reception got better and the gps started working again.

Back home, I stared at the three towers, and they stared back at me. After a while I opened my laptop, sending Jiji a response.

Jiji,
I'm so sorry to hear that. Out of morbid curiousity, what was Bradley's full name?

I closed it again and let the numb sleep of intoxication pull me into more dreams about the tower, all while the three of them stared through me.

Several hours later my laptop bell went off, startling me awake. Opening my emails, I found a reply from Jiji that was simply a link, so I clicked on it.

Bradley Joesph Long, 24, of Forest Lake, died August 18th, 2005.
Bradley was an outstanding debater, a champion distance runner, a
talented photographer, and was much loved by his many friends. Precious
son of George and Jennifer; loving brother of Sarah and Toby. In lieu of
flowers, contributions may be made to the American Foundation for
Suicide Prevention. Visitation 5 to 7 p.m., Friday at General Assembly
of God Church in Forest Lake. Funeral service 10 a.m., Saturday
August 25th, 2005 at the same location.
To plant trees in memory, please visit the Sympathy Store.
Published by Star Tribune August 20th, 2005.

My veins filled with ice, and I suddenly wondered what I had been doing. The haze of hangover had me zoning out, reading and rereading the obituary over and over again. What was I after?

But then those eyes were on me. I looked over and the three towers stared into me. Into my soul and I knew it was too late.

I still needed to know. But I hated it.

Putting my laptop down, I stood on the couch and grabbed the photograph by the frame, throwing it across the room. It crashed into the wall with a popping impact as shattering glass rained down onto my hardwood floors.

My neighbor pounded on the wall.

Tearing down the other two images I crumpled them up and threw them behind the couch as I sat, staring at nothing. Being observed by nothing. For hours. Eventually, I got up to pee and grabbed another beer. When I returned, passing the shattered frame, I noticed the writing. On the back of the photograph.

44.71702879191867, -93.08077755827959
Portrait of a Red Tower - Hank Chakowski

I pulled the location up on my phone and it was only a thirty-five-minute drive south. Heading out to the car, I couldn't believe that I was finally going to see it.

It followed as I drove in the early morning light. In every reflection, around the corner of every street I passed, hanging way back on each block as it faded away in my rearview. It followed.

Before long I was pulling off a single lane country highway and onto another endless gravel path, only now the trees off to each side slowly became sparser and sparser until there was virtually nothing around me. After a couple more miles it poked out of the horizon line ahead of me, growing in size as I approached.

A hazy, ominous sensation gripped my throat and I found it hard to swallow; hard to breathe, until I was close enough to get out of my car and witness it.

The red tower was almost bursting through the earth, as though it was being expelled. And though it wasn't too tall, it also seemed to pierce into the sky, wounding it. Everything was wrong. The scale was strangely too large and too small. The area was truly desolate, and as I ran around the fucking thing, I saw no entrances or windows or access points of any kind. Like it had been sealed away from the world.

I pulled out my phone and snapped a picture, returning to my car to swap it out with a tire iron. I was going to get into the damn thing, no matter what it took.

Walking around the tower, I tried my best to find a spot to press the sharper end of the tire iron into, but there wasn't much. Eventually, I settled on pressing it between two random bricks. Pushing and smashing and grinding it between them until I was out of breath, and nothing came from it. Frustrated, I threw the iron as hard as I could off into the distance. It landed in the gravel with a dull thud.

I leaned against the building, eventually sliding down it and ending up in the dirt myself, where I sat contemplating my next move. The tower sort of leaned into me, like it sensed my presence, but I couldn't tell if I was delirious from dehydration, exhaustion, mania, or all three.

The tower looked through me the whole time. I felt it, but it also started to become oddly comforting. It still gave me chills, but it was better than the nothing I'd been feeling for the past several years.

Returning to my car, I sat down and looked at my photo. It was exactly like the one Hank Chakowski had taken. Identical in my mind, at least. The tower on the screen and the tower looming above bored into me, peering into each and every part of my psyche, my soul, my person, and I stared back until my legs cramped and the sun was down and my exhaustion pulled me into sleep.

I awoke inside the tower. Just as in my dream, but not. The machinery was humming perfectly and there was no fetid water or hydraulic fluid on the floor. And I wasn't alone.

Others were there. Also working, also maintaining the

machines and keeping the place running. We all had our jobs, and we all knew them inside and out.

Though I had only been there a second I knew exactly what to do. And the tower stared into me, and I stared back into it, forever.

ALL ALONE ON THE STAGE TONIGHT

MADELEINE WATCHED HERSELF MOVE IN THE GRIMY MIRROR. Under the dim lights, her reflection was distorted, more shadow than human. Like the memory of a person. A ghost. She studied the way her flowing outfit shifted, tracking every twist and extension of her body. In the bloom of full light, she would have found the wings gaudy and over the top, but in the shadows they were perfect. And she knew they would retain that mystery with the distance of the stage.

It was difficult to admit it, but Pierre had done stellar work on these costumes, and on time, even--for once. Not something she could normally say. Over the previous season, he had gotten himself in over his head with projects and didn't deliver most of the finished costumes until two days after opening night, leaving many of the men on stage in thin tights without codpieces, exposed to a chucking audience.

Albert was particularly mortified, screaming at Louis, the play's director, that if they didn't come through the next day he would walk. They didn't, but he didn't stick to his promise, either. Such is the power of Jourdain's work. It draws you in, speaks to your soul, and eventually, you give your whole self to it.

Madeleine had seen what that power could do to people. People who weren't careful, people who took it all for granted,

people who became transfixed by the words and the movements and the spirit of the stage. It was a drug, a religion,
even.

She'd had a taste once, herself. On a cool spring evening,
in rehearsal for a performance of one of Jourdain's previously
never attempted works, *Mort par Mille Petits Ports*. She'd had a
few glasses of wine with the cast prior to the rehearsal, hoping
to loosen up and let the muscle memory work unencumbered.
Not close enough to opening night to matter the way those
last few rehearsals matter, but they had also run through it
enough times that they all knew their movements and lines.

Head swimming with cheap Merlot, Madeleine watched
herself from a distance from the outside, her body moving
gracefully, her mouth speaking the words perfectly. She
reminded herself of the dolls she played with as a child.

Out behind her childhood home, there was a small grassy
hill that she would sit atop and make her tattered toys dance
and jump and sway and fly. They all had names, many of
which she'd long forgotten, but Meriel was her favorite. An
angel and the most valuable thing Madeleine owned. A gift
from her father, acquired on the business trip he went on
prior to his death when she was four. Receiving it was one of
a small handful of memories she still had of him.

On that hill, out behind her house, Meriel brought
Madeleine and her father together, across time and space,
spirit and flesh. And every time, Meriel moved perfectly.

So did Madeleine on that night. Assured elegance and
confidence. An eloquence of movement. A beautiful conjunction of music and the human form. But as the performance
went on, something changed in her. Her face grew tangled
with conflicting emotions and she no longer was in charge of
her movements, well beyond muscle memory. Like a spirit was
riding her, hurtling her towards a dark, seductive unknown. It
carried her, no matter how much she fought. Terror gripped
her lungs with sharp claws and sweat beaded down her
aching back.

Madeleine's skin was on fire, her head swimming with

wine and dance and this foreign phantom. It wasn't until Louis called cut after another performer drunkenly fell off the stage that the spell broke and Madeleine crashed back into her shaking body.

Exhilarated and terrified, she ran off the stage in tears, promising herself that she'd never perform drunk again. There was an animal frenzy pulling at her, something primal and ancient; unknowable--yet familiar. Sensual, even. From that point on, whenever she was on stage, she could feel it, like it was whispering to her from the balcony, like it was watching her, angling to get in again.

More than muscle memory, more than the spirit of movement or a bacchanalian reverie, it was alive. She'd read hastily scrawled notes in the margins of various Jourdain scripts over her tenure at the theater. Others had experienced it too, though she wasn't sure who. Messy scribbles on brittle yellow paper from the distant past, performers who had likely moved on or retired or died.

At various times, they'd all been taken by something. And perhaps, she thought they might be once again.

Albert tried to comfort her that night, but he was drunk and obnoxious, trying to kiss and caress with creeping hands. Madeleine threatened to cut his dick clean off and he left her alone after that, but not before telling everyone that she was a whore. From then on, the obtrusive and malignant nature of his presence instilled in her a desire to not just maintain sobriety at practice, but anywhere, for fear of running into him.

She could generally avoid him easily, aside from practice. The script tied them together as lovers, and without quitting and sacrificing everything she had done to get into a leading role, she wouldn't be able to rid herself of him for the time being. Pleas to Louis to fire Albert went unheeded, but fortunately he was willing to forgo practicing the climactic finale kiss until the show actually began production.

That eased her nerves a bit, despite the inevitability of having to be close to the monster, but it didn't bring the peace she sought. The mysterious call still lingered for her, some-where deep inside her mind.

Back in the dim lights of the room, she watched her wings flap in the reflection, confident that she would fully embody the rebirth of the night. That she would be a guide to the dark of the unknown for the audience. Her black bodysuit gently danced with a subtle sparkle, a touch she herself had added after Pierre had given it to her.

Donning her black mask, which covered the top half her face, and double checking her lipstick in the mirror, Madeleine's stomach lacked the butterflies that typically came on the opening night of a show; that typically arrived prior to any performance. There was no anxiety, only acceptance that this show would mean something. Not just for her career, but for the audience. For theater in general.

The air was different tonight. Everything was open and inviting. She was one with all things and they were one with her; like her costume had given her new life, new connection. Something had awoken inside her.

She thought she might accidentally fly away and never return to the filthy gutters of Paris.

With a smile she walked out of her dressing room and into the back of the theater. The rest of the cast were waiting for the handful of stragglers that Madeleine was among. The room was vibrating, and the noise of the anxious audience penetrated the layers of heavy curtains.

Louis tried to calm them all, to strike at the heart of their fears and give wings to their passion.

You are here, and now you shall do what you came here to do. Jourdain has given us his piéce de résistance, if you will, with L'Appel du Vide du Vide. If we must collectively jump into the abyss in the name of the theater, then so shall we. If we must cry and sweat and bleed for the theater, then so shall we. If we must give ourselves up to the spirits of movement and dance and poetry, then so shall we.

The gravity of how he said the words imparted them with an almost biblical importance. Like Moses coming down from the mountain with the commandments, screaming God's holy writ at a ragtag group of hardened sinners found worshipping the false gods of industry and money and moving pictures.

Stagehands pushed dirty cups into everyone's hands. Madeleine looked into the cup where hazy brown liquid swirled. It smelled of apricot and tobacco, flowers and young grapes. Then a bit of burn hit the tip of her nose, making her eyes well with tears.

I know we don't usually do this, but tonight is a special one. Please drink with me, let yourself become one with the theater. Go my children, go and make perfect art. Salut!

As one, the rest of the cast downed the surprisingly decent cognac. Madeleine continued to stare into hers. On the fringes of her mind, she could feel it pulsing, edging towards her. The drive, the phantom, the spirit, whatever it was, it called out to her to submit. To let go. If she was completely honest with herself, she did want to. It was terrifying, but also exhilarating. The sensual, the romantic, the bacchanalian all spoke to her deep inside of her soul. This is what theater was; this is what art was. Poetry made as movement and spectacle, to touch the hearts and souls of others. There was no higher calling. No nobler pursuit.

Shoving her fear into the back of her mind, Madeleine gulped down the abrasive liquor, embracing whatever might come next. A warm line extended down her throat and into her stomach like a slow fuse. Playfulness overtook her as she reminded herself that there was nothing to be afraid of. This was only a play, only an audience. There was nothing else going on but passion and art. She breathed in and out, centering herself before taking her place among the rest of the actors.

Before Madeleine could react, hands were pushing her-- pushing all the actors--onto the stage and into position. A vacuum grew around her. The swell of the music and the hum of the audience became distant and thin. They were worlds apart. Her thoughts swam around her head, difficult to catch in the warm haze of alcohol.

Madeleine's costume no longer felt like she was wearing it.

It had become a part of her, an extension of her. She was a bat woman. A bringer of secret knowledge, a guiding light in the dark unknown. She straddled the worlds while others stayed in one or the other.

Looking around, the stage was now a sparse forest. Trees peppered the landscape and miles of sideways rolling black hills extended behind her. Off in the distance ahead there was nothing but darkness, as if she stood near the edge of the world and the endless cosmos were merely a single, terrifying step beyond.

Then a blinding light hit her face, blocking out the endless dark, and the shadows of branches in the sun lay upon her body like a gaudy wallpaper pattern. The shadows were so real that Madeleine tried to touch them, but her hands were gnarled and knotted. Leathery wings hung off her bony arms, connecting to her torso. Black fur covered her body, speckles of silver hair jutting out occasionally, giving a shimmering glare back in the penetrating sunlight between shadows.

There was no panic, no fear. She finally knew who she was; what she was.

An awed hush rang over the forest and Madeleine recognized that she was no longer alone. Or maybe she had never been, she simply couldn't remember. Tangled among the trees were other creatures, not unlike her. All manner of strange human/beast hybrids. A fox-woman with unnaturally long limbs, her arms damn near touching the dirt. Her ears were mangled and tattered. A hole in her cheek exposed bloody teeth and unhealthy gums.

Next to her a toad-man hunched over, not quite on all fours, but the weight and angle of his body threatening to force the position. He teetered as if intoxicated. His long, slimy tongue hung out the side of his partially opened mouth, harshly rubbing against row after row of jagged, yellowed teeth.

The contorted face of another came into the light. A twisted horsehead sprouting off a wide, bulbous body. His beautiful, elegant movements betrayed the tortured smile he carried. Arms and legs stiff like wooden poles, and yet such grace. Shadows of branches clung to him as he moved, as if they were a part of him. The sun's harshness did nothing to dissuade his exquisite movement. He came closer, and closer, and closer to Madeleine.

They all did.

A shadow followed the group towards her. Its darkness towered over the rest of them. So dense, it threatened to blot out the sun, and the unending cosmos beyond it. The group stopped as it closed in, steps taken in unison, subtle movements working in a rhythm Madeleine couldn't hear or understand.

Face to face with the horseman, the crowd parted, making way for the imposing shadow. While its movements lacked the grace of the horse, they weren't without their own particular beauty and cadence. The figure twirled around Madeleine, revealing itself to her in flashes.

Wilted limbs, then a swollen eye, then a scar-covered chest, and a starving open mouth. Bits and pieces of him revealed themselves to her, before he abruptly shed his shadow and an ancient goblin stood before her.

Recognition itched in her mind, but she couldn't place it and his large, inflamed yellow eyes stared longingly at her. A spark between them grew into a flame as the vacuum around them swallowed everything. The forest was silent, but for the sound of Madeleine's breath.

Lifting his pallid green hand, the miscreation touched his filthy finger to her lips. Contact sent a bolt through her body and the room changed momentarily. They were on a stage in front of an audience, and alcoholic vapers from his breath kissed her nostrils. But then they were back in the forest, surrounded by creatures.

It wasn't right. But Madeleine couldn't place what or why. Primal desires grew inside of her. Not of lust or passion, but of revulsion. This foul thing's hand upon her face. A small memory crept in of something familiar having happened before, but she couldn't grasp it. The thought came as the shadow of a vague and fleeting sensation. Anger and betrayal; pain and isolation. Shame.

Unsure of what to do, she leaned into it, letting the revulsion build towards the yellow eyes staring at her, pleading for her to embrace them back. But she couldn't; wouldn't.

The vacuum vanished with the crash of a deafening rhythm that came out of nowhere, filling the forest with racket. Madeleine's chiropteran form moved amongst the throng of creatures, all to the pulse of the noise. As one body, they writhed and danced with ease and refinement, like a well-oiled machine. Her body no longer her own.

She tried to stop but couldn't. Fighting against the spirit guiding them, against the shadows and light, against the movement and the cadence they collectively shared. Flickers of another life manifested in her mind, but it was intangible; inescapable. This is what was now, and what had once been was now gone.

She couldn't fight it, so she gave in. From a distance, Madeleine watched herself sway and frolic with an elegance she never knew she had. The spirit possessed her--possessed them all--and she watched in horrified curiosity as it took them.

A memory bubbled up, a small angel in her hands. Human hands. Soft and little, uncalloused by the world. She held a figure upon a grassy hill, making it bob and weave with assured nimbleness in the warm breeze. The memory brought sorrow. Despair, even. Great loss shook through her as another memory crested upon the first. This one of her father's hands. Rough and calloused, worn down by work and the weight of her world. But in those hands, he held the most beautiful thing she'd ever seen. The same doll. The same small angel that would bring her so much joy her whole childhood.

She looked deeply into her father's grey eyes. They held so much love, but also so much exhaustion. And then he was gone, and it was just her and Meriel. And then Meriel was gone, and Madeleine stood alone. Alone on a stage, surrounded by beasts in front of an awed audience. Lights shining brightly right in her eyes. The shadows of artificial trees dancing across her.

The goblin, the shadow. Albert. Standing in front of her, trying to press his lips to hers. An electric current went through the room as the audience could feel the palpable tension; the expectation of passion and frenzy and a meeting of the sensual. Poetry and theater and romance and hope.

As Albert's lips came closer, trying to meet hers somewhere in the space between them, she let herself return to the place she had just been. The forest and the creatures; the vibrating center of rage that had built up inside her for so fucking long.

Madeleine held a sense of power she didn't know she had. Her leathery wings flapped in the subtle breeze and her black and sparkling fur warmed her torso. She let the intoxication of what she was becoming grow and course through her soul. Both halves of her existed in one place and at one time. Standing in a forest and on a stage. Draped in a costume and covered in fur. She was all things.

Without thinking, without reacting, she grabbed Albert by the face and sunk her teeth into the meat of his neck. Hot, salty blood coated her mouth and ran down the back of her throat. Gnawing at the meat, she was glad she had finally let loose, after being so goddamn vigilant for so long. It felt good. This was theater. This was life.

The only thing that overpowered the cries of terror from the others on the stage, were the cheers and applause of the audience.

MESLITHE

The hallway smells subtly of rotting blood and heavy incense. Tacky flourished carpet lines the floor, littered with cigarette burns and years of skin flakes. Pointing to a door to the right, near the end of the corridor, the agent says, "That's the spot!" and inserts the key like she's immune to the smell. The smell Mark can taste. Not just on his tongue but lingering in his nostrils. Hovering in his mouth.

A man walks by, and she introduces him as Jeff, the caretaker. He smiles awkwardly, his skin gray and strange. Mark's own goes taut with goosebumps.

It's a building he'd driven by time and time again, never stopping to wonder about the units. Never stopping to think about the people who might live in them. Just another 6-unit building in a city of thousands. Old brick, built in the 1920s. Storefront talking up the majority of the main floor. Basement washer and dryer, $1.50 a load, quarters only. As South Minneapolis as it gets.

Stepping in, the wood floors creak under his weight. It's a relic of the era, where they didn't have specialty nails for the subflooring. Another classic feature, along with the brass painted radiators, solitary large closet, tiny kitchen, miniature bathroom, and single living space for the rest. Four-hundred square feet at most.

Small. But in budget.

The agent is still talking, highlighting features like the gas stove—also tiny—and built-in breakfast nook, which takes up half of the kitchen. Mark's mind wanders, taking in the surroundings but not the words.

Karen's casket at the funeral. The terror in her eyes when the aneurysm began. How quickly she was fine and then suddenly on the floor, bleeding out inside. A secret hemorrhage. A hidden purge of life and love and future. Truly unknowable.

Unforeseeable. Irreconcilable.

And if she was here now, standing with him in the dingy studio apartment just over a mile from their home, then they wouldn't need to be here at all. They would be living their lives. Together. Reaching further into that future. Deeply building that past. Instead, he's here; a walking crater. An open wound. Pieces missing and no one to help find them, much less put them back together.

But she's gone, and financial reality has necessitated moving to a cheaper apartment. Death takes so much from us. Demands so much.

It's strange how quickly things change.

The agent is still talking. Before she can finish her thought, much less the whole tour, Mark says, "Ya know what. I'll take it."

Paperwork.

Background check.

2-weeks of waiting.

Damage deposit and first month's rent.

Before he knows it, he's moved in. Only the essentials are brought with. Bed and clothes and laptop and kitchen shit and the couch and the stereo and meager record collection and a box of old books and a lamp and a framed tintype taken of he and Karen two weeks before she died. The things you need to stay alive. There is no energy, no time, no emotional ability to go through everything—to go through her things, the detritus of a life lived and left; a life built together—

before moving happens. It's all boxed up and stored at her parent's house in a spare room they don't use. They promise not to touch it. Everything on his schedule.

His *grief* schedule.

First night is quiet and uncomfortable. Unpacking alone, setting up his new life. His widowed life. It's too much. Tears and labored breathing on the kitchen floor. Pleading to nothing and no one. Begging her, wherever the fuck she is, to come back; to not be dead.

He wants to scream, but his voice is raw and dry from sobbing so hard, so long. Tears run until there's nothing left. They always come back, but the time spent after they're gone—either numbness or some kind of brief acceptance or simply unable to cry any more—is the best it ever gets.

Cleaning himself off in the kitchen sink, the water runs hot on the cold and cold on the hot. Mental note made. By the time he gets it perfect, just warm enough to bring the life back to his salt-licked cheeks, the water starts flowing out thick. He avoids it, luckily, as it splatters into the sink with the texture of cold, congealed gravy. Putrefaction and iron fill the room. He cuts the faucet off and texts Jeff, who's number is scrawled on a note on the table in the breakfast nook, alongside a copy of the lease and a spare set of keys.

Minor revulsion replaces the numbness, and he cracks the kitchen window, cursing himself for not having checked the water pressure on the tour. Best get some jugs of water.

And some bourbon.

Walking vaguely toward the natural food co-op with the liquor store across the street, he is suddenly standing in front of their old house. *My old house? Our old house.*

New tenants must have moved in, the lights are on, and various furniture and boxes are still on the front porch. Shadows move in the windows. The 2nd floor of an early 1900s duplex. Also classic South Minneapolis. Wood floors, radiators, dark wood built-ins. Their home for 10 years. His home for 10 years. *Theirs* for 9 and change. Despite the movement within, it seems so empty. So lifeless.

If only he could have figured out how to make it work, how to stay living with the ghost of their future. With her ghost. He imagines her walking through the house, in spectral form, not being able to find him; being surrounded by strangers and their lives. Torn apart by death, and then again by capital.

If only she could be here.

Tears threaten to come, but his body is fresh out, so the numb wraps around him like a cloak and the feeling of wasting away climbs into his heart. It's cold; so fucking cold.

His feet lead him to the co-op, where he avoids old friends and neighbors. Anything to not have another person tell him how sorry they are. How special she was. How much they, too, miss her.

The liquor store is a different story. Just an assortment of anonymous, random people. It's socially sterile and impersonal. Exactly what he needs. He grabs a bottle of Laphroaig 10–Islay, her favorite region–and puts it on his overloaded credit card, grateful when it goes through. Partner death is fucking expensive.

The closer he gets to the apartment, the more real it becomes. The more real it becomes, the more that sickly feeling develops in the bottom of his stomach. Sidewalks paved with litter, marked by drunken piss, and covered in broken amber glass lead the way. *Home?*

No.

But it is, now.

The building looms over him. Looms inside.

He pauses before finally entering. The hallway still stinks, but maybe he's getting used to it, as it no longer coats the inside of his mouth. Thoughts of Karen carry him to the door, what little tears he has recently produced threaten to spill over his eyelids.

Key in the lock of his front door and his phone buzzes. A text from the caretaker. *Out of town for the weekend, will look when I get back. Welcome to the building.*

Mark threatens to reply *It's fucking friday* but dissuades

himself from doing so. *I guess no showers for the weekend, and more jugs of water to cart home tomorrow.*

As he's stepping inside, the door opposite of his opens. She stares at him. Almost through him. Tattered dark brown hair. Low-key goth-punk vibes, like she's over trying too hard. Arcane symbol on her black shirt, more tattooed on her arms and legs. Dark eye make-up.

For a second, she takes Mark's breath away. Not because she's beautiful, but the way that she's beautiful. So similar to Karen. Not uncannily so, but enough that it hurts. This happens on occasion, walking down an unsuspecting street or wandering through the grocery store. Somewhere totally normal. Someone unexpected. Always. It never fails to melt the circuits in his brain for a second; be it a passing resemblance, stylistic similarity, a matching movement pattern, or a doppelganger laugh. Never intentional on their part, always emotionally crippling for him.

Trying to compose himself, tears threatening even stronger now to break their confines, she speaks first, which Mark is eternally grateful for.

"New neighbor, right? I'm Wren…" A pregnant pause follows, while Mark clears his throat, trying to conjure the words. Any words. Brain still a scramble of harsh reality and fading memories. "Hi, I'm Mark," squeaks out, nearly a whisper.

Eyeing the bags, "You too? Water's been weird all week. Must be grand having just moved into this dump, huh?" She continues before he can reply. "I've got some cold beers and a couple bottles of booze if you want to stop in. I can tell you about the neighbors…"

Mark lets it hang for a moment, on the precipice of not wanting to have to say no, but not exactly sure that he wants to either. "Or another time, if you're busy right now…" She gives him the out, graciously. He turns toward his cracked door, weighing the options. "Fuck it, gimme a second," comes out of his mouth. He's as surprised as she is.

"Perfect. Door'll be unlocked. Make yourself welcome

whenever you want." With that she turns and disappears into her unit. Mark stands in the hallway, collecting himself. Dual shards of isolationism and desperation for distraction tear through him like he's nothing.

He sets his bags down on the couch and heads to the bathroom to splash water on his face in the hopes of returning some blood to his cheeks, or getting some of what's there to disperse, he's not quite sure which it is he's feeling. The water comes out thick and gray just as he's about to put his hands in it. He turns it off and grabs one of the bottles, thankful that he was lost in thought when he turned it on. Rinsing his face helps; helps ease the burden of his life as it is. Helps ease the burden of having to make decisions in a new life that he is wholly unprepared for.

He leaves the bottle in the sink. A reminder for the middle of the night.

Almost out the door he sees the brown bag with the scotch inside. *Always rude to visit someone empty handed…*

Gently knocking as he opens Wren's door, Mark is shocked at how sparse her apartment is. Same size and layout, but mirrored against the central hallway that cuts their apartments off like a vein. A bare mattress on the far side of the room with a loose sheet swirled at the bottom. The minimalist bed nestled snugly in the corner by the lone wall with windows and the kitchen door; radiator at the foot, almost touching it.

Battered couch with a cardboard box sitting next to it, shadeless lamp on top, the lone source of light in the main room, enhanced only by the kitchen and bathroom lights cascading in. Dim, but not overly so. A smally, rickety bookshelf on the other side of the couch, to the left of the kitchen door. Full of books, magazines, and various ephemera. Mark doesn't recognize any specific titles, though they're all difficult to discern in the low light. A short, oval-shaped wooden coffee table sits in front of the couch. The top is stained, warped, and damaged. Chips and cuts, chunks and uneven areas where the top veneer surface has been peeled back and broken off. A few label-less empty beer bottles sit atop it. A small stereo is against the wall with the door to the hallway. Turntable on, needle popping and hissing as it spins in the alley groove of a record.

The wall opposite the couch and table, nestled between the doors to the bathroom and the lone closet, a floor-to-ceiling collage affixed to the wall. No way to remove it without dismantling it piece by piece or destroying it. Wren's voice from the kitchen, "Make yourself comfortable, I'm just getting something together for us."

"I brought scotch, if you want any. I know you said you had booze, but force of habit built in from my wife...my late wife." The words cut him. Still getting used to saying it. Not *wife. Late wife.* There's some sense of ownership with the words, like it makes it more real and that's oddly important to him. To not deny it, to not run away. To confront it head on and accept her death. At least that's how it is today. Every day tells its own story.

Hesitation from the kitchen. "Oh my god, I'm so sorry to hear that..." she trails off at the end, clearly unsure of how to react. Mark knows he's new at this still, but not too new to know the exact feeling of that reaction. The uncertainty of what to say: let it bounce off, like the person typically wants it to, or dig in some. Both options are awkward.

Just a mild, "Thank you," followed by, "This collage is amazing, your work?" He leans in to inspect it, unsure at first what he's even staring at. The images collectively form a blurry figure almost, one wrapped in a tube—*maybe?*—but it's hard to tell if that's intentional or not. Below the figure, is a dark pool.

Looking at the detail, not the overarching form, reveals a different story altogether. The entire collage is made from porn. Vintage from the look of it. All varieties of hardcore. Straight, gay, lesbian, bondage, all body types and skin colors represented. Dicks, fingers, dildos, tongues, fists in every possible opening. Some moan with pleasure, others pain. Restrained and unrestrained. Indoor and out.

A wall of fucking.

It's strangely beautiful.

Transfixed by it, not erotically so, but by the magnitude and care taken to erect a shrine to all-out fucking, Mark misses Wren entering the room, two empty low-ball glasses in one hand and two labelless brown bottles in the other. "Yeah, I spent the better part of my first year living here making that. Took a lot of time to get the…to get it right, ya know? The right feeling of it."

She hands him a glass and sets the beer down on the table, grabbing the scotch. "Ooh, Laphroaig, solid choice," she pulls the seal open, pops the top, and takes a deep whiff of the smoky liquor, pouring two fingers in her glass before offering to do the same into his.

"Thanks. How long have you lived here, if you don't mind me asking?"

She shifts to the couch and Mark follows suit, sitting down and letting the abrasive 70s fabric irritate his elbow skin. It's a comforting, familiar sensation that brings him back to the basement in his parent's house when he was a kid. Often ignored, placed in an extra room full of storage, and an old TV someone had given them. Eventually a second VCR found its way to them as well. When opportunity arose, Mark would sit on the couch and watch VHS tapes either from their meager collection, or checked out at the library

It became a place of refuge, safety. Isolation.

Wren's voice interrupts his memory. "Oh, a while. I'm not great at counting back the years, but I've lived here for quite some time. Longer than anyone else, at least." She half-laughs at the end.

The scotch is smoky and complex, but hasn't yet opened up, which sends a shiver down Mark's spine. "Didn't catch you for a rookie," she laughs this time, in earnest, and passes Mark one of the bottles.

"Thank you. And for inviting me over. Sorry it was weird for a second. I…my wife passed recently. It's been… hard." He pulls his keys from his pocket as he speaks, using his church key to pop the caps off both. "Sorry. I don't mean to dump all that on you. We don't need to talk about it. In fact, maybe let's not talk about it...I don't know. Sorry."

She takes a sip of the beer. "It's ok. I'm...sorry. Uhh...so a friend of mine brewed these beers. He lived in the apartment in the basement. Good stuff, huh?" A slow smile crawls across her face as she rises and flips the record, filling the apartment with warm synth.

Mark, after taking a hearty swig of the beer, "Oh cool. It's solid stuff. Pilsner, right?"

"So he says...said..." she pauses. "So, like, we don't have to talk about it, and I don't bring this up to make us talk about it, but I guess you put your recent loss out there, so here's mine. That friend died this year. The one who made this beer...I took what was left from his kitchen and am slowly drinking it. I don't mean to make it weird, just thought you should know you're drinking dead man's beer...I mean, I don't think it matters, but I don't know. Pain for pain, I guess. Shit sucks, huh." She trails off.

Mark takes another swig of the scotch. It's smoother than before, like a minute amount of air has gotten into it and loosened it up, though it's probably just that he's had a little. "I'm sorry to hear about your friend...Life is fucked, huh?"

"Cheers to that!" They clink glasses together, both emptying them, before Wren pours them refreshers.

"Since I'm the eldest tenant, I mean in terms of how long I've lived here, how about I tell you about everyone else who lives in the building? So down the hall from us, on my side, we have Martin, who I literally never see. I think he works nights or something. Quiet older man. Seems nice, but in the few years he's lived here, I've seen him all of maybe a dozen times. Across from him, who you share a bathroom wall with, is Terri. She's a delight. I'm honestly surprised she hasn't stopped by with cookies or some other home baked good. She's lived here almost as long as me.

"We don't see as much of her as we once did though, as

she's getting up there in age and has some medical issues, but if you see her be sure to say hello.

"First floor is just Jeff, the caretaker, who I'm guessing you've already contacted about the water, but if you haven't you should. Chill guy, just don't cause any problems and you'll be ok."

Mark's eyebrow raises instinctually.

"No, no, don't worry," she laughs," mostly like don't get so drunk that you pass out in the stairwell. That kind of thing. Since that abandoned storefront takes up the rest of the main floor, he's the only one down there.

"There's also the basement unit…but that's…that's still empty. No one down there since Saul passed." She looks away, out the window. To be anywhere but here.

Mark knows the feeling all too well.

"I'm sorry. So, is…uhh…the water a normal occurrence, or is this new?"

Slamming back the rest of her scotch and pouring another, "Happened a few times lately, I'm not sure. Best bet is to keep some jugs of water on hand. They think it's deep down in the pipes and are probably going to keep putting band-aids on it until a fix becomes absolutely necessary."

Mark takes a large swig of the beer. It's yeasty and thick. Earthy in a way he's never experienced before. Almost callow, like it wasn't allowed to ferment long enough, yet not wholly unpleasant. It cools him down, moving through him like ice water. Things become easier, for the moment. The sobbing heart inside is quiet. Not silenced, but no longer at the focal point of his thoughts.

A shaky peace.

Several drinks later and their lips are locking together, tongues skipping and swimming across each other. It doesn't feel wrong or hard or strange, it feels like oblivion. It feels like darkness and silence.

They pull each other's clothes off, an awkward dance of pent-up sexual frustration, pain, loneliness, and a desire for connection. Anxious mouths meet engorged genitals, hands grasping and groping, teasing and fondling. The air between them humid and alive, their pain stripped bare and left scattered across her apartment. The bed calls to them, pulling them down. Wren pulls Mark into herself. He shudders. She writhes. Breath hot and quick, unbalanced, unrefined. Skin upon skin, flesh inside of flesh. Teeth on lips and ears and necks. Nails like claws across rugged canvas. Muffled moans heard down the hall.

Her buckling to a finish triggers his, unprepared and unconsidered, they just let go into each other. The rough fibers of the bare mattress scrape against his sensitive skin. The last thing he remembers before everything goes dim.

A hazy moment in the middle of the night. The jaunt of her breathing gently moving the sheet atop them. Eyes heavy, not exactly open, but not closed either. A figure standing above, at the edge of the bed. Earthen and sour. Something dripping. A soft squishing sound, then silence.

Morning sun hits like hot pokers in his eyes. A foul taste lingers in his mouth and his bones ache. It takes him a moment to remember where he is, what he did last night. He heads to the bathroom to pee and rinse out his mouth. His urine splatters into the bowl with a syrupy consistency, and sits atop the dense liquid already there, but he's too busy rubbing the sharp crust from his eyes to notice. Pissing feels strange, but not alarming, so he never looks down.

The flush sounds odd and squelchy, but he's too busy remembering to not use the faucet. Walking to the kitchen, he takes quick appraisal of the place. Empty. Wren isn't here. *Must have left for work?* He checks the cupboards for bottles of water, but there's nothing. Not even food. The fridge is full of bottles of Saul's beer. That's it. *She must eat out a lot…*

Questions don't stick for long under the pressure in Mark's skull. He throws on his clothes and walks across the hall to his place. Pouring a glass of water from one of the jugs, he then slams the whole thing in one gulp, before pouring himself another, which he drinks more reasonably. Then he cleans his face with the jug in the sink.

He sits on the couch and drinks more water, begging the universe to take the headache away. Down the hall a door slams. One of the other neighbors. The unseen person is walking down the stairs. Pressure builds inside and he bursts into tears. Hazy visions of holding Karen on their wedding night, exhausted and elated and the future brimming with so many vibrant possibilities. It shreds him. So callous to fuck someone else so soon. He knows it's ok, that she would want him to find connection and joy and anything else he could, but there's just emptiness inside.

She once told him that if he died first, she would pack up all their stuff and move to the Pacific Northwest. Start again, crammed into a tiny apartment surrounded by their things. New life, new job, new city. Living a new way in the wreckage of the past.

The opposite of what he's done. Through tears, he chuckles. Of course; they were so fucking different.

The tears abate, numb wrapping him in a shroud. He wipes the wet from his cheeks, but they're tacky. In the bathroom mirror, dark gray streaks down his face. Clumps of goo in the corners of his eyes. *The fuck?* He works it clean with a damp towel, which does the trick, but provides no answers.

Then everything slows down. Sluggish. His muscles atrophying on his bones. Joints stiffen and inflame. He manages to hobble to the bed, crashing down upon it. His thoughts try to race, but they too are slow, bizarre. Like he's connected only by a sliver. Darkness overtakes everything.

When he awakes, the sun is coming down. His rigid joints have settled, and he isn't in as much pain, but his body is different. Its movements and sensations dulled and muted.

He stumbles to the hallway, hoping Wren can help. As he walks he grows limber, strong, and the bizarre feelings pass. *Maybe I just slept weird. Too much to drink?*

Wren's door is fully open with the place still empty, but an unopened Saul beer sits on her coffee table with a note.

Grab this and come down to the basement, I have something to show you...

Seems wrong to assume it's for him, but it's also not out of the realm of possibilities. Since she told him about Saul, he's wanted to check out the basement, beyond the laundry room. He grabs the beer and heads down. *Fuck it.* His mind floats as he opens the bottle and takes a swig. Grief, desperation, thoughts of Karen all tucked away somewhere silent.

A door, opposite the far side of the laundry room, is open, dirgey post-punk music echoes out. Mark follows the sound and saunters into the room, taking deep pull of the earthy beer as he enters.

Wren is in the middle of the space, dancing to the rhythm of the music. It's one big room, gray painted concrete floor and crumbling old walls. They're lined with rickety shelving stacked with wooden cases of bottles of Saul's beer. Thousands of them.

As the song winds down, she stops dancing and drinks a whole bottle in one chug. "I feel so fucking good. So alive." She smashes the empty bottle into the corner and dances more as the next song creeps on. Analog synth, warm tube guitars, repeating dubby bass-lines.

"I love this song. It just moves through you. Like a spirit…"

He pulls heavy from the bottle, watching her dance. Reminded of Karen. Then a twitch in his brain, like a muscle spasm. His vision blurs. Sweat coats his body, like shock.

The room twists as Mark is pulled to the floor. His legs jellylike and soft. His breath bizarre and hot. *What the fuck is happening to me.* The thought comes out garbled, a murmur on his shaking lips.

"You're such an easy fuck. So desperate and pathetic." She laughs and her voice warbles and distorts. Something creeps in behind her, sticking in her shadow on the floor and wall. Intersecting with the shelving and boxes. Gloom made solid.

Suddenly, Mark is being dragged to the center of the room, shadows to his left and his right release him and stand near Wren.

"Oh yeah, you've met Terri, and that's Martin. They're your new neighbors!" The pair stare down at him, crooked smiles on their wrinkled faces. It takes a moment for Mark to register what's happening. Terri, the agent who showed him the unit, stares deeply into his eyes. But she's older, impossibly so.

"He doesn't get it, guys!" Wren stops dancing to belly laugh. As she does, the shape behind her moves into view. Not shadow but not solid either. The silhouette of a man cast in rotting Jell-O. Lumbering and shaky but formed together. It almost slides toward Mark. Pieces drip off around it as it moves.

The door to the room slams shut. Caretaker Jeff waltzes in.

Wren again, "Well, looks like we're all here."

There is no ceremony, no prayers or incantations or lit candles. No reading passages from ancient texts or invocations of primitive gods. The shape is upon Mark, forcing itself inside his mouth and nose. Makeshift fingers first, then a whole malleable hand and forearm. Before too long it's shoulder deep, shrinking and convulsing to maneuver itself deeper. Mark is choking, trying to gasp for air, but there's nowhere for it to enter. Other limbs invade his ears and eyes.

The mass writhes inside of him, silencing his fight or flight. Rooting around in his mind and body, trying to ride him like a horse. Mark resists, but now he's seeing everything. The full truth. Wren and Jeff and Martin and Terri and dozens of others. Prior eras, all of them young and beautiful, just in different styles of clothing, going back decades and decades.

A skip forward to this city, this building. Less of them now, but all so much the same. Pulsing into the future, the mass fully inside Mark, showing him the truth in picture and emotion.

The time before. Before the followers and the building, before the city. Before people and animals. When land was scarce and there was only mounting chaos and lifelessness. He squirmed from nothing, growing and evolving to meet new needs; adapting to new worlds that came again and again and again. Worlds that are still changing and shifting and growing.

So much recent pain and loneliness and loss. And fear.

For the first time, real fear.

A corrupted body, cells multiplying in mutant ways, cutting its life far too short. No one who fit. No new usable new blood. Some of the group aging too rapidly to keep up. No longer powerful enough to keep them all young and full of life; no longer powerful enough to maintain control.

But then Mark. Ideal conditions. Broken, defeated, psyche in that same chaos. Body whole, not too young, not too old. Manipulated into to providing the proper host. Whole self prepped for this moment; a bit of slime to prime the host.

He forces his way deeper, sinking into Mark's body. Filling him with strength and vigor. Mark's grip loosens for a moment. Just enough time for the mass to grab everything, pushing him in. Like a stowaway in his own body.

The group yell and dance as he stands, triumphant. Grabbing a beer, he forces the cap open with his thumb, splitting the skin, and in a wet gravelly voice says *Cheers!* The congregants fall to their knees, lapping at the blood and slime mixture the wound creates as it drips from his hand. He tops off some bottles of beer with the sour fluid and they all drink it down greedily.

In seconds their skin grows smooth and tight. Youth and vitality return as they stretch their healing joints and muscles. Terri and Martin no longer old, but impossibly young and beautiful. Like gazelles made human. Graceful and aweinspiring.

Deep inside something moves. Mark struggles but the rush overwhelms him.

His congregants hoot and celebrate with revelry, chugging their bottles of beer. Drinking his very essence, like some perverse communion. Strength and power grow as he breathes in with life, adapting his form and cells into this new vessel.

Leaving his followers behind, he heads up the stairs to the second floor and enters his apartment. Beyond shock. But also, someone new now hiding within. Perhaps bringing healing to deep recesses inside. Pale moonlight cascades across the wooden floors. Mark's bones are awkward. He remembers them, but also remembers not having them. A schism in his memories; in his mind.

Mark sits on the couch and breathes, letting the scent of wood polish and acrid water ground him to the present. He contemplates the residue of his old life. Scattered pieces of something that was once so beautiful, which had been reduced to little else than pain. He contemplates the new memories he now holds, ancient and formless. The overlapping of these two worlds.

Maybe a new start. Maybe a second chance.

His eye is pulled to the tintype of him and Karen. It hurts, but not as much as it did before. The wound on his thumb drips pink slime onto the couch.

It's strange how quickly things change.

FROM THE PAST COMES THE STORM

THE DOSSAL MELTED AS MUCH AS IT BURNED. NOXIOUS BLACK smoke poured from an old wound above the altar. Gasoline fumes lingered as flames spread manically like a living organism. Charring wood creaked and screamed under the weight of the steeple above.

It was coming down.

Chris grabbed Valerie, pulling her toward the door. Her black makeup streamed down her cheeks, her eyes burning and full of tears. She couldn't shake the sound of cawing birds, hidden by the cackling flames. Chris was an apparition, known only by touch. Heard only in wheezing breaths a world away.

"Fucker lit it too fast...I wasn't fucking ready..." She coughed out the words. Not exactly to Chris, but not *not* to him either.

A pillar of smoke poured from the shattered windows, blotting out the stars. Paul was nowhere. Breathing was harder. Painful. Chris and Valerie both gasped for air. And the door was heavy. Impossibly so. The dark wood blistered their palms as they pushed against it again and again. More than resistance. Moving a mountain. The finish was both tacky and slick all at once as it melded with their skin.

With the last of their waning strength, they forced it open, leaving chunks of flesh on the hyper-heated wood and stumbling into the quiet night surrounding the blazing church.

Fresh air met the inferno, heightening it into an explosion. Flames licked Chris' cheek. His vest and hoodie threatened to fuse to his skin. Hot plastisol ink and searing cotton atop malleable flesh. Burning wood and melting polyester. Sizzling metal and boiling paint. Shattering glass. Charring flesh. Hard concrete meeting them both.

A striking figure, backlit by the flames, appeared in the open doorway. Emanating smoke, perhaps built of it. Long wisps rolled off them as they casually stepped out of the church and into the darkness beyond the peering eyes of the fire. And still the songs of birds, hidden somewhere within the church. Hidden somewhere in the heart of the flame.

Then near silence. A haze of smoke and the darkened sky. Burning everything. Anguished breaths.

Squealing tires. Cool air. Colder water. Lifted to the heavens before being placed in a moving casket.

Is this how I die? Chris wondered.

Followed by

So fucking stupid.

Labored breathing, burning lungs, and then nothing.

Behind the car's dust, the church creaked and groaned, extinguishing the rampaging fire. Waiting for daylight so it could begin to grow anew.

"THERE's that Jean Genet quote. Something like, 'I recognize in thieves, traitors and murderers, in ruthlessness and cunning, a deep beauty—a profound beauty…' I'm probably fucking that up, but the point remains." Thin fingers of smoke circle Stu in the darkness, mildly illuminated by the unnatural blue-white light bleeding in from the lone street lamp outside.

In the mostly barren room, Assück's Misery Index LP spins out in the gutter of its locked groove. Crumbling plaster reveals bare slats in the walls. Black and white photos of Kathy Acker, William Burroughs, Samuel Delany, Georges Bataille, and Genet sparsely cover the walls, the latter of which has a golden halo shoddily painted above it, crowning Genet sainthood. Chris sits across the room on an aging, undressed mattress, a swirl of sheet and blanket eternally slipping off the end. Clutching Paul's zippo, Chris stares off into nothing. As he waxes poetic, Stu remains crouched in the corner.

He continues, "Then again, there are some folks who think Genet is a villainous figure, so I guess it should all be taken with a grain of salt." He pauses for a moment to inhale from his nearly spent cigarette. A long bit of ash hangs precariously.

Chris coughs and groans deeply before drinking down half an Old Style. Fresh scars—shiny and pink—squirm atop old skin as he shifts in the near darkness.

"But there's something there right? 'Beauty in thieves' and all that? I'm not crazy for thinking we should just do this..." Stu trails off.

"Fuck man. We did it. We did all of it before you fucking got here and now I'm still fucked up and Paul is fucking dead. So you can talk your shit and have your revolution in your head, but the rest of us are carrying the goddamn scars, Stu. Not you. Fuck." Pain drips off Chris' every word, a gathering storm of anger, tension, grief, and lust.

Stu finds Chris' eyes in the darkness and locks into them, like he's prey. And Chris wants to be—mostly—but he also wants Stu to shut the fuck up. He also wants Stu to be *his* prey. Chris' irritation wanes as loaded desire and longing for something other than pain comes to the forefront.

Stu rises, dropping his leather jacket to the floor and stripping off his Celtic Frost Morbid Tales shirt, revealing a mess of blackwork kitchen-scratch tattoos. His tattered black boots scrape against the stained wooden floors as he approaches Chris, setting the glowing remains of his cigarette out on the grimy windowsill. Peeling paint jumps away from the ember as it's extinguished next to the bottle of Old Grandad the two polished off over the course of the evening.

For a moment in the low light, Chris sees Paul in Stu. It robs him of his breath. But he still wants this. He wants Stu. He wants Paul. He wants to allow both desires to exist at the same time and not detract from each other, to not let the grief own him. Stu stares down at him.

Locked eyes. Locked lips. Their beards a tangle of barbed wire. It's all the stripping of black denim, wet mouths, rigid cocks, anticipatory holes, slapping hips meeting thrusting asses. They find each other, inside and out. They find each other as they become one again and again.

Stu smells like leather, smoky wood pulp, and frenzied instinct as teeth gnash upon trembling lips. Stinging sweat, abrasive body hair, and the roughness of an uncovered mattress blend into hard flesh and bright hot blood bridging into each other. The diminution comes fast

after they both cum and the azure glossed room fades into a deep expanse of nothing.

THE DOSSAL MELTS as much as it burns. Noxious black smoke pours from an old wound above the altar. Gasoline fumes linger as flames spread manically like a living organism. Charring wood creaks and screams under the weight of the steeple above.

It's coming down.

Within the walls of smoke, Chris searches for Valerie, but she's nowhere. The cackling flames and creaking wood mute any other noises. His cries of *Valerie!* go unanswered. Through the shroud, he heads towards the door. But before he can place his hands on the swelling wood, his eyes catch something across the sanctuary.

A hazy black figure crawls from the fleshy fissure above the altar. First it follows the flow of the smoke, before breaking off from it and jumping to the melting carpet below. It's the same as what he saw before he passed out. The cry of birds follow behind them, filling the room, overpowering the screaming fire.

The figure crosses past him and he tries to make sense of it. Billowing black robes cover the hobbling thing, its face hidden by a filthy white cloth, with makeshift mouth and eye holes, stretched and distorted like a melting mask fashioned from clay. For a moment it stares at Chris; stares through him. His knees go weak as the crying of birds fill his head.

Suddenly Valerie grabs Chris' arm and pulls him out the door onto the blaze-warmed tarmac.

It happened again. How does this keep happening? What the fuck is that thing? We had a goddamn plan Chris says, out loud to both Valerie and no one before her soot-covered face distorts to a blur and the burning church illuminating them both goes dark.

Silence, again.

Heat, again.

Hands touching Chris' body, again.

Cool air and colder water, again.

Nothing. Again.

Then, in the dust behind the car, the creaking and groaning of the church shifting to put itself out. Waiting for daylight, so it can grow anew. Again.

Flames dance and flutter into the night. Wood cracks under the heat, which fights against the cool autumnal air. Valerie leans against Chris. Her sharp shoulder pressing into his bicep. She takes a pull from her Mickey's 40oz and sighs heavily. Chris pulls a bottle to his lips and drinks deeply of the fire and hand-warmed malt liquor. It seems foolish, but this is the type of moment that in other circumstances might feel like home.

Valerie continues, "...and that's when we had to come here. I fucking hate to have abandoned the rest of them, to have abandoned our work, but it was getting too fucked up out there." A tear rolls down her cheek, which she wipes quickly, frustrated.

"We were doing something, ya know? Actually doing something. For the first time in my goddamn life it felt like we were making a goddamn difference. An eventual felony seems almost worth it, but it's not like I want to get caught or anything. Shit, I'm sorry Chris… What the fuck? Paul…" She trails off, leaving the air silent between them for an overly long beat.

"Fuck, I'm such a mess. Thank you. Lori and I really needed this. We needed a place to hang away from back home. I'm so sorry about Paul. That never should have fucking happened. I should have…I should have found him."

Slow tears roll down Chris' cheeks. He drinks again from his 40oz, letting the malt stream down his throat in a single, unbroken line until the bottle is empty. It sits at the bottom of his stomach like a bag of sand. He prays to nothing for it to numb the pain, both emotional and physical.

He can hear Paul's voice, telling him about all the important work Valerie and Lori were doing in the Pacific Northwest. Their campaign of stealing HRT drugs from big pharma trucks in the dimly lit parking lots of various Fred Meyer locations. Their mission to spread those HRT drugs to other trans communities in Oregon and Washington through an underground, DIY network of punks, queer activists, and allies.

Look at what they did with so little. It's like the personal and political are the fucking same, and small rebellions are as important as giant organized ones. What can a single cell of friends do? Clearly a lot. What if we light the first match? Paul's words run over and over in Chris' ears.

Paul's words from the night before the first fire. The night before Valerie and Lori showed up on their porch, ragged and afraid. Sitting in his backyard, Chris and Valerie cry themselves to drunken sleep, wrapped in each other's arms.

CHRIS COMES to and Paul is talking on the phone. He catches bits and pieces of words before his still-sleeping mind recognizes what he's saying as a discernible language.

"Look, I know we don't actually know who threw the first brick at Stonewall—or if it was even a fucking brick. Maybe it was a rock, or a piece of wood, or a rusted piece of metal that had snapped off a passing car weeks prior. I'm just saying it started somewhere. We can be that brick. We can be the person who threw it. But now... " He pauses, taking in what the other party is saying. At one point he stammers, trying to cut in with some unintelligible words, but he's quickly silenced.

Chris fades back out, Paul's voice circling the drain in between his ears. It stretches and distorts before it's little more than a whisper. A memory. A phantom.

When Chris wakes up Paul's gone.

Chris pulls on his black jeans and Ulver shirt, which still stinks of anticipatory sexuality. It reminds him of the grave. Open and waiting for the right moment. The thought makes him wonder if he's delirious. He grabs water and tries to cool himself off.

I shouldn't have drank so much.

Before he can get himself adjusted to being awake, the door swings open. Lori carrying a backpack and a suitcase. A look of shock on her face; a distant look of all-pervasive anxiety and stress. Valerie waltzes in behind her, her skin almost green. The three embrace, hugging for what might normally be an uncomfortable amount of time but isn't. It feels like home. Security. Safety. For all of them.

Paul follows behind and heads into the kitchen to make them all breakfast while the three catch up.

Over tofu scramble and sourdough toast, while Bathory's Blood Fire Death cracks and pops on the turntable, they begin a conversation which starts with why Lori and Valerie are there, and will lead them to burning down the church.

At one point, Paul says, "Stonewall started with a single brick thrown. That changed everything. What if we did that. But here. And now. Christian fascism is coming after all of us, and others. I say we fight back. I say we light the match…"

A WEEK after the first fire, Chris, Valerie, Lori, and Stu drive to the rubble. Axegrinder's Rise of the Serpent Men drones on as they pass through the near-desolate edge of the city, into the not yet suburban area that consists of mostly farm-land and industrial warehouses. Chris' burns are still raw and tender, but they're finally getting better.

They all need to see the damage. They need to see where Paul's remains are. Were?

Since the fire, none of them had been able to find any news coverage of the arson. Or any word on a body found. The unease of getting caught came with Valerie and Lori. Now it follows Chris, too. No news doesn't seem like good news. It's ominous.

They need to say goodbye.

Driving, Stu sees it first. "We in the right spot?"

The others look up. The church is standing. Unbroken. Unaltered. Not burned. Not a pile of rubble.

Its steeple rises into the sky tall and proud. No scorch marks on the walls. No broken windows or charred wood.

Almost in unison, the three say, "What the fuck?"

Out of the car, they wander around the parish, baffled by

what's in front of them. Baffled by the irreality of the situation. Like wandering through someone else's dreams. The church looms over them, casting darker than usual shadows. Casting sinister auras.

The doors are closed. On the steps leading to them sits a single human tibia. It's clean. Not polished, but free of blood, muscle, tendon, or other tissue.

Instantly, Chris is dizzy enough that he can barely stand. *What the fuck? This has to be a fucking dream…*

Lori screams. A banshee shriek that pierces the eerie silence of the chapel before them. The church screams back. And in that scream, Paul. They can't hear it, but they all feel it in their bones at the same time, and lock frightened eyes.

Chris storms to the car, off-kilter as he jogs. "This can't be it…we came to the wrong church. It was dark and we didn't know where we were going, right? Right?" It comes out with a tremble. Then, "Where the fuck is Paul?" Barely audible through a sob.

The rest pile into the car and they speed off. Chris muttering *fuck fuck fuck fuck fuck fuckfuckfuckfuckfuckfuckfuck* under his breath as they go. Lori hyperventilating. The same look of shock riding all their faces. Glassy eyes, trembling nerves, shaken cores.

There's little planning that day. Once the sun goes down they all just grab what they need and pile into the car. Like an unspoken agreement—a deathpact, as Lori dubs it on the drive. They all have gasoline, lighters, and matches. Social armor made from black denim, leather jackets, and work boots now imbued with extra meaning. Outcast clothes ready for war. And not that it hasn't all seen it before. Knuckles on bleeding nazi faces, fists wrapped around bats pummeling abusers. Battle, yes. But not this.

Emperor's I Am the Black Wizards blends into the white noise of the wind as the vehicle careens to the other side of town. It envelopes Chris. His mind a tangle of fear, anger, grief, confusion, and single-minded devotion to the task at hand. He sees Paul's face. Pulls their lips together, like they had done so many times before. When he pulls back, Paul's face is gone and the distorted white cloth mask is staring back at him. Chris stifles a scream. Barely. No one notices, all lost in their own nightmares. All lost in the horror of what had happened, of what was about to happen.

The moment the church is in sight, the car is filled with the cawing of birds so loud it overpowers the stereo. So loud it overpowers their reactive screams.

Lori grabs her ears, trying to block out the sound and the moment she lets go of the wheel, the car swerves into the grassy ditch. She slams on the breaks before they hit an old crumbling stone retaining wall. With the jostle of the near impact the birds go silent.

Everything goes silent.

Stu tries to speak but nothing comes out. Their bones vibrate. The church is talking to them again. Peering into them. Stu jumps out of the car first and pukes. His skin, pallid and greenish. He doesn't make it more than a few steps before he passes out, thudding to the ground with a bounce. Lori rushes to him, kneeling at his side. Without a word, Valerie and Chris grab gas cans from the trunk and walk to the church.

Its doors are open. It has been waiting for them.

The single leg bone remains on the steps, no longer clean. Bits of rotting muscle and tendon dangle off it. A swarm of insects fight for the tissue.

Staring down at the putrescent bit of Paul, Chris freezes in place. A torrent of memories. The masked figure he saw before. Piles of rotting birds. The smoldering wound above the altar. His mother dying. His father disowning him. Picking gravel from his knees as a child, blood dripping off the toilet. The sense of being totally alone. Being totally alone. Then, eventually, Valerie, Stu, Lori, all his other friends. His chosen family.

Paul.

Reflections of the past two attempts ripple through his mind. *What makes us think this time anything will be any different?* he mutters over and over to himself. If Valerie hears, she isn't concerned. With a brief beat of hesitation, she waltzes into the chapel like she owns the place, a thick stream of gasoline trailing behind her.

It's enough to spark Chris into action, who follows suit. But not before picking up Paul's tibia.

Inside the church is cold and silent. Chris does his best to get as much gasoline as possible all over the unnatural building, hoping they can burn it to nothing. Anticipating burning it all again even after it has been reduced to little more than ash.

Focusing on his task, it takes him a moment to realize he's alone in the church. Well, not *alone*. Something is watching him. In a panic, he throws the can of gas towards the altar. It arches above it, raining fluid as it flies, before it lands against the far wall, below the fissure that will grow, or maybe just be revealed once the plaster burns away.

The screaming of birds fills the church; deafeningly loud. Loud enough that blood trickles from Chris' ears. Loud enough that it makes his body tremble as the sound pushes through him.

Awkwardly pulling Paul's zippo from his vest pocket, Chris lights it and throws it into the growing rainbow puddle. *Thirst for disgrace.*

THE DOSSAL MELTS as much as it burns. Noxious black smoke pours from an old wound above the altar. Gasoline fumes linger as flames spread manically like a living organism. Charring wood creaks and screams under the weight of the steeple above.

It's coming down.

Chris still can't find Valerie. A figure passes by him, encased in shadows. No black makeup streaming down their face. No coughing fits or panic. Her voice in his head over and over again, *Fucker lit it too fast. I wasn't fucking ready…* but someone else. Fingers of smoke follow, darker than those from the fire they're standing in the middle of.

They climb up the melting dossal, above the altar where the wall has crumbled and fallen away. Into the old wound.

Chris follows.

The liquefying fabric melds to his flesh, but it doesn't register. Plaster and wood rain down around him, but no heed is taken as Chris climbs up onto the altar and pulls himself through the smoke-hemorrhaging fissure in the wall. The outer section crumbles into cinder under his grip, but as he shifts himself inside, the wood grows from desiccated to fleshy and pulsingly alive.

It pulls him in with a brief sucking sound. Protruding blue veins writhe around him, dragging him deeper and deeper in. Sour smelling mucus coats him. The birds grow louder.

The walls of the tunnel press against him, squirming as they force him into an awkward crawl until he reaches a drop. Then unnatural silence. For a moment, Chris' ears are full of the beating of his heart. No. Someone else's. Overpowering. His legs slip out of the tunnel. It's not a chamber he's going into, but a sudden drop. His stomach hits his throat. He struggles to grasp onto anything, but it's all too slick. Gravity brings Chris down into the darkness below.

He lands with a thud and a crack as his shoulder hits the ground first. Stars. The room is moving. So many stars. As he staggers to rise, sweat pours off him and the stars grow brighter. Chris settles himself on the ground for a moment, catching his breath. The wet, stagnant air tastes like copper and rot. He stifles a gag, which makes him shudder.

More stars.

More sweat.

Debilitating shoulder pain; clavicle pain.

The antechamber is like the inside of a hollowed out tree. Slimy wooden walls, made not by man, but by nature. Or maybe something else. Dark, patinated brass veins weave in and out of the walls and floor, their surfaces undulating and rippling in an unheard cadence.

Chris rises again, this time carefully so, and stands without stars or sweat. Every time he shifts or moves, the two broken ends of his collarbone grind against each other. It's agony, but he presses on.

There's an opening at the far end of the room. As he crosses the threshold between them, the droning of a thousand out-of-tune pipe organs rings out, all playing the same funeral dirge in different keys and microtones.

Writhing brass roots stretched out in front of him endlessly. The walls a combo of crumbling wood, mildew-covered stone, and blood-rich dirt. Occasional streaks of gore litter the ground. Jagged bits of bone and tissue protrude from the wood and soil of the walls and floor.

The massive room smells putrid and earthy, with an undercurrent of rotting blood.

Chris crosses to the halfway point of the room. Tunnels sprout off from every wall. Then he sees the birds. They're perched, unmoving atop a pile of decomposing human tissue, flesh and small bones. They grow louder the closer he gets, but never move.

Standing in the center of the chamber. Chris isn't alone. The figure looms behind him.

Before he can pull the tibia from his vest pocket, it's already done.

Filthy skeletal claws sever his throat. Quick, but not clean. Tattered shreds of skin dangle off multiple deep wounds. Bits of muscle stick to the claws, as they bring it to their gnarled mouth.

Before he fades out, the figure stares down at Chris. Chris recognizes the drooping face, not as a mask made from cloth or stretched and sculpted clay, but rather human flesh and bone.

Twisted vines of brass pierce through him. Weaving him into the floor. Taking from him, but also leaving something else. Deep in his heart. The cries of organs vibrate through him as he leaves his body behind.

THE DOSSAL MELTS as much as it burns. Noxious black smoke pours from an old wound above the altar. Gasoline fumes linger as flames spread manically like a living organism. Charring wood creaks and screams under the weight of the steeple above.

It's coming down.

Valerie rushes near the flames where Chris disappeared. The fissure pulses and squirms. *Did that fucker really just go in there?* She calls out his name, trying to overpower the fire, collapsing building, birds, and the bizarre organ lilt that seemingly came from nowhere. But it was no use. No way he could hear her. She could barely hear herself.

She had to get out.

Then the steeple caves into the church, flaming wood raining down atop her. Valerie doesn't have time to scream.

Lori watches the church collapse in on itself. Stu remains out cold. At his side, she knows her friends are gone. No one could survive that.

She also knows what they had come there for.

Grabbing her and Stu's gas cans, Lori deftly stokes and spreads the fire from the outside. Hoping to make it burn for as long and as large as possible.

The church groans and shifts, but she keeps pace, splashing it here and there, lighting downed tree branches and tossing them into the blaze. Anything to keep it going. Anything to weaken it.

Birds and organs and endless screaming fill her ears, but she knows she must do it. She knows it won't stop her. She runs around back and kicks in the rear door, causing the inferno to explode, flames licking her face. *This is for you Paul. Chris.*

Valerie.

Tears well in her eyes. But she keeps adding and reigniting. *Don't mourn, organize* repeating over and over in her head.

Eventually the temple is little more than a pile of rubble and ash. She reignites that too, until there's little else than smoldering cinder.

As the morning light crests over the horizon, Lori crams Stu into the backseat of the car and drives away from the cursed sanctuary, leaving a trail of dust in her wake.

Off in the distance, below the ashen heap that was once a church, an ensanguined brass sprout blossoms from Chris' chest, and the church begins to grow anew.

THE ANTECEDENT

My eyes traced the darkened shades between the two figures, as I had done every day since I found the painting in Paul's things. It was nestled between other pieces of art he had made, some finished and framed, like this one, and others left abandoned, forever. This painting was from his period of experimenting with oils, though I'm not exactly sure when it was done. Likely college, sometime before we met.

Housed in a rough, antique wooden frame, two stags with their antlers intertwined, stuck together. One was standing, looking off to the side. The other appeared dead, its limp body drooping onto the grass and rocks below the standing figure, its head dangling under the weight of its body. This wasn't triumph or victory; this was destiny. It made me feel sick the first time I saw it.

In the year since he died, I fixated on the painting, going over every detail of it without concern for knowing why. It pulled me in, over and over again. Every time I walked by it, I had to stop and study it. There were days where it felt like that painting was the only thing keeping me going, the only thing keeping me from ending my own life and hoping to see him again. But there were days where it felt like it was the only thing other than my sorrow that even existed anymore.

There were other days where its appearance filled me with dread and confusion.

This wasn't the only painting of his in the house. My life was surrounded by his art. So many paintings adorned our walls before he had died, and I hadn't been able to even think about taking any of them down. But the other paintings didn't make me feel the way this one did. None other crawled into my smoldering chest cavity and took residence.

Visually, the painting was arresting. Stark use of vibrant colors made it seem unreal behind the glass. As I stared at it, I wondered why he had never shown it to me. In our nearly ten years of being together, how had I not seen this. Every other piece of art in that pile I had seen, at the very least in passing. The confusion could momentarily stifle my tears, but they always came back; as did the overwhelming sense of unease.

Widowerhood is one long string of days spent trying to run down the sunlight and make it home without crumbling to dust in front of everyone. And then it's one long string of nights spent tossing and turning, alternating between ugly crying until there are simply no tears left and the sort of anger that presses on your heart the way coal is crushed into diamonds. It's exhausting, and horrible, and so fucking boring. I pivoted between being emotionally dead and sobbing all the time. And nothing ever helps. The one person who could help is dead, and no longer can we wrap our arms around each other for comfort and love, because he's in a fucking box in the frozen soil.

Staring at the painting became my comfort. I began to lean into the uncomfortable feelings it provoked from me, spending hours staring at it, tracing my fingers along the dark shadows and lines, focusing my pain on the tangled web of antlers. This was my meditation, my reprieve from suffering; or, at least, my acceptance of it and its inevitability. And like meditation, at times it brought me great peace, but other times I walked away shaken and disturbed; almost like my soul was waking up.

Entire days were spent staring at the painting. I even hung

it near my bed, so I could sit comfortably and gaze into it; so that it was the first thing I saw when I woke up. The more I looked, the more questions I had. Without him here to answer my obsessive questions, I turned to a few of his friends from college. The outside world was bristly and made me raw, so I invited several of them over for drinks on his year and three-month deathiversary.

I had been seeing less of them; less of everyone. There was a guy I had been having an undefined, physical relationship with just before I found the painting, but I had ended it. The loneliness was no longer something to contend with, it just was. I stopped returning phone calls from my family, I had stopped returning phone calls from Paul's family, not that they called much; really it was only his sister. My own friends understood, I think, why I had become so distant. But the well of self-imposed isolation still hurts; it's still isolation.

Before they came over, I brought the painting into the living room and hung it near the couch. I wanted everyone to be able to see it; I was curious if any of them would have similar reactions as I did. But the night came and went, with no one showing up. Not a call, not a text. Just the lonely, empty house I had barely left in months. Perched at the edge of the couch, a whiskey on my lap, I cried myself to nothingness.

The next day, I took the painting down, covered it in a blanket, and put it back in the second bedroom closet next to his other old paintings and his clothing. It was like cauterizing a wound; every nerve crackled and singed. My vision blurred on the edges and tears streamed off my chin and onto the hardwood floor below my feet. Like every other painful step, this had to be taken. I needed my life back.

For some widows and widowers, the distraction is booze, or drugs, or shopping, or work, or sex, or tv, or exercise. For me, it had become staring at the twin stags. While it made me think of Paul, it didn't make me think of his death. Like all those other distractions, it never completely covers, it only pulls the eyes away from the worst of grief. I suppose it's odd that my reprieve came in the form of something that was very much of my late husband, but it made all the sense in the world to me.

Putting it away allowed me to resume grieving. I started interacting with the world again, slowly, when I could. Outside no longer felt as painful. For a while.

Over the next few weeks, my mood increased mildly on a curve, before crashing down again.

Isolation.

Comfort.

Separation from the outside world.

Then the phone calls. Voice messages. Texts. Emails.

Seemingly everyone, all at once. Needing me. Wanting to see me. Asking me to go places. As if after the first year and change everything was fine. As if I was over his death. Like it was some hurdle I had jumped and now my life and emotions would return to some pre-widowed state.

I slumped onto the couch and cried until there were no more tears, only streaks of dried salt on my cheeks. He was dead and I was alone and there was nothing that would ever bring him back to me. Nothing that would ever unify us again, in spirit or in flesh.

The interlocked deer flashed in my mind.

In a desperate plea to feel him again, I got it from the back closet, uncovered it, and hung it on the wall in my living room. It called to me. As I gazed at the painting I had spent so many hours studying previously, my stomach filled with napalm. The dead deer had begun its rot, parts of bone and skull now exposed under tattered hide and darkened flesh. The living stag was no longer triumphant in battle, but weakened, laboring under the weight of his defeated opponent, his unnatural conjoined twin. It was different.

Wrong.

My knees trembled as I stared into the now feeble stag's eyes. I was fucking losing it. Every part of my body and soul were wrong, but I just couldn't give into the fight or flight; I was too exhausted. Because he wasn't here, and I was.

Because he should fucking be here. Because fuck him for dying.

And fuck me for ever having thought that.

The tears poured out of me like hemorrhaging blood, coating the floor in front of me with drying salt-stains. The world made no sense after he died. My entire life made no sense. There was nothing ahead of me. All there was left was pain and sorrow and loss and grief and a lifetime without him; without the one goddamn person who meant more to me than myself. I had nothing. I wanted to become nothing. I wanted to join him, forever. But I couldn't. I knew I couldn't. The pain, sorry, loss, grief, and loneliness enveloped me like a cloak. This was my armor.

Struggling for air between sobs, I pulled myself onto the couch and slept. Delirious dreams of ancient forest gods distracted my mind from the sorrow as I trembled through my sleep. For most of the night, I wasn't aware if I was sleeping or awake. My living room, the forest in which old gods battled until I blinked and there was nothing but the dull morning light.

Sweat drenched my clothes and seeped into the couch cushions, so I made my way to the bedroom. My bed swallowed me whole and whisked me away to the black void of nothing. No dreams, no tremors, no stags. Nothing; sweet and total nothing. It was the first time I was close to him since he died.

I awoke sobbing, gasping for breath. The room was stuffy and dark, tear stains covered my pillowcase. Crawling from the void, my clock bafflingly reading as nine at night. I slept for an entire night and then all day. My head was full of molten lead, my brain simmering in it. The tears stopped rolling down my cheeks.

The painting in the living room, seemingly mocking me. Impossibly staring into me. Rotting deer, more desiccated and gone. Little more than skeleton and the thick, dark ooze of long rot. The living deer, barely standing, its skin taut against visible bones. Blood trickled from its nose, eyes, ears, and mouth. Pink froth littering the browning grass carpet below.

Paul's unmoving hands. His lifeless form in the open casket. His unopened eyes. The pallid skin, gray and dull. It all poured into me; poured out of me. All the shock. All the pain. All the sorrow. All the rage. All the terror.

All the fucking silence.

I threw the painting across the room. Its glass shattered and the frame burst apart upon impact.

Before it found peace upon the ground, I was out of the house, the door slamming behind me. I ran into the woods behind our house, hoping to lose myself in them. Hoping to vanish, or be swallowed whole, or find a portal which would never take me back to my miserable existence.

My soles clomped on the hard-packed dirt of the lone trail running through the woods from our backyard. When he was alive, Paul spent a lot of time back there, trying to get the lay of the place; trying to figure out officially-unofficially where our property actually ended and the County's land began. It was a futile effort without the help of a professional surveyor, and ultimately didn't matter, as our house butted up against a section of woods that no one seemed to care about, much less know about.

It was a dense forest, stretching back for at least a couple of miles, eventually melding into a wetlands area full of swarms of black flies and not much else.

Running on adrenaline, shock, and every single irrational thought and impulse I'd suppressed since Paul died, I pushed deeper and deeper into the woods. My shins screamed at me. My lungs fought for air. My head tingled. But I kept running. Through the pain. Within the pain. The house was wrong. The painting was wrong. My whole fucking life since Paul died was wrong. And there was nothing that could change that part, so what if I just kept running.

Eventually my body gave out. My legs frozen and my lungs burning, I was forced to stop. Trembling muscles pulled me to the ground. I was both so weightless that I floated above the ground and so heavy I sank into the damp earth. Vision blurred with tears and sweat, the humid air like a wool blanket. I laid in the dirt until I could feel beyond the pain; when the muscles loosened and my breathing became almost normal.

Fresh focus on the world, on my surroundings, revealed the world in dark greens and rich brown. Crickets chirped off in the distance and something cried over the forest. I turned my head in the direction of the howl. My brain caught the scent first, before it even registered in my nose.

Foul and rotten, the sickly-sweet smell of decaying flesh. My heart jumped. The lingering scent drew me in. Through a cluster of tightly grown trees, in the middle of a small irregular opening, a deer carcass sat in the center. Areas of it still swollen and bulging with the gasses of internal rot. Other sections dry, almost mummified. Giant antlers sat atop its skull. A perfect, unbroken layer of shimmering white velvet wrapped around them. Pristine. Untouched. Free of rot or decay.

Vacant orbital sockets stared into me. Deep into my loss and brokenness. Without words it spoke to me. Not in voice, not in my head, but coursing through my body; shuddering up my bones.

Salvation.

Without words, I bent down, my inflamed knees creaking and screaming, and pulled the rotting cervine corpse up, leveraging as much of it on my shoulders and back as I could.

The stench of ancient rot with an almost floral perfume undertone cradled me in its arms as I struggled to get the beast positioned correctly. Brown-red innards splattered on the dirt below and yellow ooze snaked a trail behind me as I walked.

Within the intensity of the decay and the pervasive and overpowering scent, I found comfort; true comfort. Like wounds closing rapidly inside.

And yet everything deep in my mind was screaming that this wasn't right. That it was all terribly wrong. I walked home, rotting deer carcass hefted upon my shoulders, in a dreamlike daze of hope and healing. It carried me as much as I carried it.

In the irreality of it all, I never noticed that despite its condition there wasn't a single fly or maggot or any kind of bug. Despite its rottenness, it was immaculately unpolluted. Untouched by the natural world.

Reaching the house, my lungs rattled under the weight of the beast and the distance home, I gently got it into the house and waited until I was in the bedroom to set it down, right onto Paul's side of the bed. Its gangly limbs hung off the side of the bed, pink-yellow stain slowly spreading on the fitted blanket atop the mattress.

My muscles were immobile; every part of me aflame and spent. Crashing down on the couch, I stared off into nothing, centering myself. That small voice deep inside still cried about how wrong this all was, but exhaustion had brought it to a nearly inaudible whisper. Pieces shifted inside me.

Paul, standing before me on the day I proposed. Tears in his love-fill eyes. The way his hand felt in mine as I slid the silver ring on. Us holding each other; both that day, and the day he died. Him walking out the house with a smile. Never seeing him alive again.

The way his body lay limp on the stainless steel table in the morgue the last time I saw him. The respectful movements of the mortician. His even breath. Paul's lack thereof.

Emptiness.

Suffering.

Shock.

The deepest loneliness I can even imagine.

My eyes moved to the mess on the floor. A trail of mephitic fluids from the door to the hallway. The painting on the floor; shattered glass and broken wood. The deer, once again bizarrely, impossibly altered.

The lower stag, a clean skeleton. The upper, past the point of living. Gaunt cheeks, gravity having successfully pulled it to the ground; its position mirroring the skeletal one.

Dark blood pooled below its frame. Still locked in struggle. A cycle of triumphant-defeat made whole, as the twin stags lie in death together.

Their empty eyes stared into me. Stared through me. And my body wanted to violently tremble, but inside there was a newfound calm. Beyond the irrational, beyond the PTSD, beyond the death, grief, and mourning. A sense of security and safety.

There was no guilt about feeling ok. There was no added shame or fear that it meant I had lost my connection to Paul. For the first time since he died, I was ok.

These thoughts led me into the bedroom. I turned off the light and laid down on the bed beside the deer. It groaned as I got comfortable, hissing out its nostrils once I stopped shifting around with the blankets.

The rhythm of its breathing lulled me into the most restful sleep I've ever had. One of pure silence and nothingness. One of universal oneness.

A return to my mother's womb.

The following morning I woke up weak and groggy. Despite feeling the deer shift in the darkness, it remained how it had been when I fell asleep. The yellow-pink stain had expanded below it. Rubbing thick crust from my eyes, I stumbled into the bathroom and looked at myself in the mirror. A ghoul stared back at me, with deeply sunken sockets and anemic, gray skin. My joints were swollen and groaned audibly as I moved.

Yet I radiated tranquility. Like a monk with a life spent entirely in a meditation practice. Their body distorted and malnourished, but their consciousness expanded to the point of enlightenment, and beyond.

I was in that place.

Gravity pulled me back to the couch. The deer's breath following behind me; following inside of me. I traced back the mess. The line of rot from the door to the hallway, no longer rotting, but replaced with sprouting floral buds. Sweet perfume lingered atop the sickly smell of putrefaction.

In the corner sat the painting, its splintered frame and shattered glass coated in a thin layer of fresh moss. The twin deer stared back. The skeletal deer had regrown its muscle, skin, and patches of fur. New life glowed in its eyes. Determination, or something approaching it.

The previously triumphant deer was bloated and rotting, its eyes gone, the sockets filled with maggots. Swarms of flies hovered around it. Their antlers were still locked together, but the sense of weakening bone radiated off the now-dead deer, like they might snap off under enough force.

My stomach lurched and my body trembled, but my mind was resolute that this was all correct. Necessary. Desirable. Unavoidable.

My phone vibrated loudly on the coffee table. An alien and forgotten sound. I picked it up to see 46 text messages and 24 missed calls. The screen was blurry and hard to read, words indistinct and fuzzy. I set it back down, wanting to avoid whatever was happening in the outside world. I was where I needed to be. I was focused on what I needed to be focused on.

The deer sighed heavily in the other room and my heart palpitated with a radiance of love I haven't felt since Paul died. Wholeness of being. Peace of spirit.

Floating to the bedroom doorway, I peered in at the deer still decumbent on the bed. Its chest rose and dropped in cadence with its warm breath. The yellow-pink had grown to cover the entire bed, no longer a stain, but a pool. Flowers peeked beneath the surface of the fluid.

My arm the was resting against the wall collapsed, my flesh tearing like crepe paper; the bones beneath shattering into a dusty gray powder.

Serenity.

Both my knee joints popped out of place, sending me crashing to the floor. The yellow-pink pool poured over the sides of the bed, spreading onto the wood below. It spread so quickly. My hip shattered on impact. If I wanted to cry, there were no tears. If my body wanted to go into shock, there was no sweat. Like all the water inside me had been drank by another.

Tranquility.

Without water, the body shrivels and dies. My skin split and cracked open. My eyes dried up, as did every mucous membrane. My phone vibrated in the other room. Distant sounds of pounding on a door. It didn't matter.

The fluids of life met me on the ground. Flowers replaced my eyes; roots replaced my nervous system. My flesh, a blanket of perfect soil for the sprouting grass. I became one with the nothing, with the everything, as hooves clattered upon wooden floors.

It was love.

The painting, thick moss obscuring it, now showed the formerly skeletal deer standing triumphant, its antlers free. Below the other deer was barely visible, reduced to little more than a pile of new growth; broken antlers poked out of the grass between vibrant purple irises.

THE STILL BEATING HEART
OF A DEAD GOD

I walk through the front door of the trailer. Again. Same door as every day. Same door in the morning, same door at night, alternating in versus out. Or out versus in, maybe. I don't think I know anymore.

I walk through the door. Beer stains on the olive green shag carpet, cigarette burns on the patterned upholstery of the itchy brown and orange couch.

Buckled and ripped away wood paneling on the wall. A layer of fake brick behind it. A layer of off-white wallpaper behind that. Like someone needed to know what was behind each layer but got bored after the second revelation.

He's still there. He doesn't think I can see him, but I can. His eyes watch me. His disappointment almost bubbles over, but he controls himself. He always controls himself. I'm half-convinced that he only controls himself because he thinks I don't know he's there. The argument he wants would reveal him, so he just sits and watches.

A lot like he did before.

His spot on the couch is still indented, that's how I know he's there. His subtle shifts and jerks alter the dents in the ancient and likely crumbling foam padding of the couch cushions. I'm tempted to lay across the couch with my feet up, as though to stretch them across his legs, but I never do. I always just sit next to him.

I walk through the door. Not sure if it was in or out this time, but I'm standing in the entryway, or what we called an entry way at least—with a small two-by-two square of linoleum surrounded by olive green carpet on three sides, front door on the other. He would want me to kick off my boots so as to not track snow and salt and mud into the house, but he's not here—or at least I pretend like I think he's not here—so I keep them on just to spite him.

Things were like this when he was here, too. Or rather when he knew that I knew he was here. When I could see him and hear him. When he would snore so loud it would shake the walls. When he would scream and throw the crystal ashtray I bought for him at a garage sale when I was in the third grade. An early birthday present.

It would dent and crack the cheap wood paneling, leaving an impact point of splinter and remnant ash. But the ashtray itself never had so much as a scratch. Still doesn't, sitting on the coffee table in front of him. The one with wood veneer peeling and buckling. The one covered in Stroh's cans. The dark blue ones with the lion crest on them. The ones I haven't moved since he left.

Or since I thought he left, at least. Since he wanted me to think he left. Since I realized that he hadn't left but want to maintain the illusion that I think he has.

I walk through the door and am standing on the square of torn linoleum and he's not just looking at me, he's looking through me, like I'm not even there. Like that time he forgot me at the grocery store. I walked home. He was pissed.

I walk to my room. He's still pissed.

My bedroom is the same as it was when I was seven, which is the same as it was when I was seventeen, which is the same as it was when I was twenty-seven which is the same as it is now.

Narrow like two hallways next to each other. One slightly shorter than the other to make room for the closet that's to the left of the door in and out. Single bed along the shorter hallway. Dresser at the end with a black and white television atop it. Bunny ears atop that. Dust atop that.

I pull the knob to turn it on but there's just static and noise. It wraps me in analog warmth so I leave it on. He fumes in the other room, just another ghost in this mausoleum.

The thought falls from my mind as I get into the dusty bed and fall asleep.

Gears clatter and shift in the night, pulling; trying to pull me awake, but I stay locked in the quiet cool of nothingness until the morning light is cascading across my eyes through the broken blinds covering the single window of my bedroom. A violent cough erupts from my lips and I jolt upright, struggling for breath.

There's nothing in the other room. It's too quiet.

I head out, still coughing. My arms are covered in smears of sweat and dust, which I accidentally transfer to my face. In a fleeting glance of the bathroom mirror, I look like a hobo-clown.

His spot is still there, molded into the fabric of the couch, but it no longer shifts. He no longer stares. He no longer judges.

I grab a Stroh's from the warm, horrendous smelling fridge, and sit down at the filthy dining room table. Stacks of bills and plates and bowls with ancient remnants of things that once resembled food take up the entire surface at all but the one placemat intended for the solitary vinyl seated metal chair.

It creaks as I sit down.

The beer opens with a snap and I take it down in two slugs, letting the can become one with the decor.

Without thinking, I get up and walk through the door and am standing in the living room again. This time the television is on. Not the one in my room, but the one next to me. And he's staring at me.

For the first time since he left, or at least since he thinks I think he left, I stare back. Not through him. Into his eyes. Into the voids that have been staring at me, observing me, judging me, trying to understand me, since the day I was born. The voids that I've been pretending like I don't feel on me every single time I'm through the door. Or back through the door. Or wherever I am and however I got here.

No walls, no feelings, no masks, no covers, no distance, no county borders or state lines or swaths of land or geological formations have ever been enough to keep those eyes from watching.

He stares back. Into mine. Not through them. Into them. Like he knows I know he's there. Like he knows I've known he's still there. Like he knows I've been pretending to not know he's there.

We go on like this for a while until my empty beer can on the overloaded table falls to the floor and breaks me from our staring contest.

The rats are back again.

I walk out the door and I'm in the same place. Or is it different this time. Hazy film-worthy memories of our lives together play out in front of me. The trailer is mostly clean, but as time goes by it get progressively more filthy and dilapidated. Progressively colder and more alone and more desperate and more disconnected and more anxious and more prone to contemplations of suicide.

I don't just see it, I feel it. What it does to your heart to feel abandoned. What it does to your body to give up. What it does to your soul to be encased in bitterness and all the what-ifs and why-won'ts of the rotten world.

I walk back through the door and the trailer is the same as it was when I left. And he's sitting there in the permanent groove of the couch and he's staring at me, and maybe for the first time in a very long time I don't see judgement or criticism or disappointment but rather I see sorrow.

And all I have in that moment is remorse.

ACKNOWLEDGMENTS

First and foremost, Jes. For everything. Also for giving this book its title.

My sister Kari for all the ongoing support and help with this weird, fucked up endeavor.

The Void Collective: Edwin Callihan, Matthew Mitchell, O F Cieri, Justin Lutz, Charlene Elsby, Michael Tichy, and Evan Dean Shelton. For keeping me sane.

Brendan Vidito, for giving edits/notes on virtually every one of these stories. I couldn't do this shit without you.

Everyone who originally saw fit to publish these stories and helped carve them into something beautiful: Ira Rat of Filthy Loot, Mae Murray of Medusa Publishing Haus, Scott Dwyer of Plutonian Press, and Evan St. Jones of Heads Dance Press. Support these small presses.

And finally a long ass list of writers/publishers/friends who are far more deserving than being omitted by accident. You know who you all are. If we talk books, stories, publishing, events, marketing, bullshit, life stuff, sad stuff, hard stuff, you are the best and I'm only here because of your help, support, and friendship.

Finally, my dad. Sorry I didn't get this out in time for you to see it. Thank you for everything. Love you forever, pops. See you around.

PREVIOUS APPEARANCES

Earlier versions of these stories previously appeared in the following publications.

- The Spiraling Cadaver originally appeared in *Feral Architecture: Ballardian Horror*, published by Weirdpunk Books.
- The Nest Within originally appeared in *Teenage Grave 2*, published by Filthy Loot.
- Body Alone originally appeared in *The Pinworm Factory*, published by Plutonian Press.
- Flesh Crucifix originally appeared in ltd capacity in the chapbook *3 Hits From Hell*, published by The Void Collective.
- Jizz Christ originally appeared in *Stories of the Eye*, published by Weirdpunk Books.
- Portrait of a Red Tower originally appeared in ltd capacity in the chapbook *All Will Writhe*.
- All Alone on the Stage Tonight originally appeared in *Let the Weirdness In: A Tribute to Kate Bush*, published by Heads Dance Press.
- Meslithe originally appeared in *Soft Ceremonies*, published by Filthy Loot.

- From the Past Comes the Storm originally appeared in *The Book of Queer Saints 2*, published by Medusa Publishing Haus.
- The Antededent originally appeared in *Fucked Up Stories to Read in the Daytime*, published by Filthy Loot.

ABOUT THE AUTHOR

Sam Richard is the author of *Grief Rituals*, *Sabbath of the Fox-Devils*, and the award-winning *To Wallow in Ash & Other Sorrows*. He has edited ten anthologies, including the cult hits *Profane Sorcery* and *The New Flesh*, and his short fiction has appeared in over forty publications. Widowed in 2017, he slowly rots in Minneapolis where he runs Weirdpunk Books. You can stalk him @SammyTotep across socials or at weirdpunkbooks.com

Profane Altars: Weird Sword & Sorcery - edited by Sam Richard

In the spirit of Robert E. Howard, Tanith Lee, Karl Edward Wagner, and films like *Conquest* and *Fire & Ice* comes *Profane Altars: Weird Sword and Sorcery*. Underground horror authors Emma Alice Johnson, Matthew Mitchell, Adam Smith, Sara Century, Charles Austin Muir, Edwin Callihan, and editor Sam Richard conjure forth visions of the unknowable and ancient past. One of spider gods, aging warriors, crystal antlers, cultist soldiers, and whispered legends of strange creatures and woeful knights. A bridge between weird horror and Sword & Sorcery, *Profane Altars* presents new realms fantasy within cloistered worlds of doom and wonder.

Featuring cover art by the legendary Jeffrey Catherine Jones.

Infinity Mathing at the Shore & Other Disruptions - M. Lopes da Silva

A heartfelt, disquieting collection of short stories focused on body horror, transness, anti-capitalism, queerness, decay, transformation, living buildings, rot, ruin, vintage arcade games, and so much more. With *Infinity Mathing at the Shore & Other Disruptions*, M. Lopes da Silva has solidified themself as an essential and sharp voice in the canon of 21st century queer horror.

Cover art by legendary punk artist Croad.

www.ingramcontent.com/pod-product-compliance
Lightning Source LLC
Chambersburg PA
CBHW030900200726
48289CB00003B/840